Though The Brightest Fell

The Brooklyn Angels Series
Book One

Nola Cancel

Printed in the United States of America

First Edition Printing, 2017

ISBN-13: 978-1546334538

Though The Brightest Fell

The Brooklyn Angels Series
Book One

ACKNOWLEDGEMENTS

Thanks is never enough—

First and foremost, to my family who created this strange creature who prefers to live in her head and write about the people she finds there.

To my nieces and nephews, you have given my life meaning and more love than I will ever deserve. To those with us, those no longer, and those yet to come, I am proud of you all and love you more than words can say.

To Susan, for many reasons, but mostly for always being there.

To my father for the tools and my mother for the strength.

To my online family and friends, especially Granny Goodwich, and the brilliant author Greg Wilkey, thank you for the friendly ears, kind words, and the unwavering support.

To my editor, Todd Barselow, who helped a 54-year-old computer illiterate achieve her dreams—no matter how big a pain I am.

To AR, what can I say that I haven't said before? Your support, your willingness to answer my questions—no matter how inane or how often—and your constant and gracious encouragement in my darkest hours have given me a strength I never knew I had. There is no novella without you.

To my husband, Michael, the man who has stood by my side for the past 30 years. The guy who came home one day with a weird story of a nondescript storefront with two words in the window—Stress Relief—and the immediate discussion that led to this novella. For the authenticity, for the humor, for the journey through your childhood memories, this book is as much yours as it is mine. Love forever and always or until we kill each other (whatever comes first), your Nola.

PROLOGUE

And God said, 'Let there be light,' and there was light.

But this light kept getting brighter and brighter as it raced toward Joe DeFalco.

Walking out of the bar, after three beers and four shots of Johnnie Walker Red, along with the four or five Percocet he'd taken before leaving his house, Joe was feeling no pain. He also never noticed the delivery van as it ran the red light on the corner and came barreling straight at him.

Perhaps, if he had noticed it, he might have been able to get out of its path. Now, it was too late. Joe was a dead man.

The last thing he remembered before everything went black was the smell of fresh cut grass on a beautiful spring day and a feeling of euphoria that Joe assumed everyone felt at the end of their lives.

"Sweet Jesus," he said as the light enveloped him...and the light was good.

CHAPTER ONE

Azriel woke up to complete darkness. Something was obscuring his vision. If he were any other creature, he might have thought this was an after-life. But, as an angel, he had firsthand knowledge of what humans could expect after they died, and this was not it.

His enhanced hearing caught tidbits of a conversation that could have easily come from two rooms away or two miles away. Not yet used to so many voices all at once, the accident had left him even more disoriented than when he'd first arrived on Earth.

Right before the accident, his senses had been bombarded by all the noise and filth of this world. The barrage was almost more than he could bear and might have explained why he was so ill prepared for the force and ferocity of the truck that hit him. Perhaps, he should have studied more about earth and 'its inhabitants.

He tried to move, but could not. He was being restrained. His limbs felt heavy and he could no longer release his wings. Whatever held him, he knew two things for sure—it had been used on his kind before, and he was in trouble.

CHAPTER TWO

Joe slurred, the heroin working its magic on his body.

"You're outta your fucking mind," John said, tapping his tied off left arm and looking for any good veins left to hit. "There hasn't been a real angel sighting in sixteen years. And that poor fucker didn't make it through the trials, much less distribution."

The basement was cold and damp and smelled of mildew and age. The two childhood friends had been using the basement of Joe's parents' house to get away from their lives for years.

After his father's death and the fall that left his mother unable to care for herself, he and Nan had moved into the old place.

Despite its memories—or maybe because of them—Joe still preferred the basement to the rest of the house. No matter what was going on in his life, the basement offered solace in the guise of forgetfulness. The pills and heroin didn't hurt either.

Joe smiled as the fog set in. Soon he wouldn't need to rob Nan for money or get his shit off the street. The source of all his fixes for the foreseeable future was tied up in his laundry room. This angel was his lotto ticket, and the payout was better than anything money could buy. From now on, his own piece of heaven was right here on earth.

"You'll see, John," Joe said, as the soothing waves of numbness began to envelop his mind and body. "Before long, we'll have our very own angel essence empire."

CHAPTER THREE

The unloved were not a group of kids whose parents didn't want them. The unloved were fallen angels. Cast out and abandoned by God here on earth till the end of time because they refused to accept God's rules concerning his mortal children.

According to the unloved, humans were worthless and should be treated as nothing more than excrement beneath their feet. They believed that angels were, and always would be, superior to men. Unlike their heavenly brothers, the castoffs refused to accept the fact humans were the most beloved of God's creations and were given the gift of a soul because they were so favored by the Lord.

To make up for their unfair treatment, these hopeless and abandoned creatures had made it their business to inflict as much pain and death on the "meat-bags"—their name for humans—as they could possibly manage.

This penchant for making humans suffer had, more often than not, been thwarted by the careful watch of their brethren still loyal to the lord. If not for their steadfast vigil, humans would constantly be in danger.

In fact, the unloved considered their protection of lesser beings the ultimate act of betrayal, and therefore took great pleasure in destroying any of their heavenly brothers here on earth that they found engaging in such treasonous activity. This was not an easy task.

When an angel came to earth on a mission, they were forced to assume an earthly form. With a few mind tricks, they could hide themselves from the easily manipulated humans, but their angelic powers made them practically invulnerable. Both of these factors made it next to impossible to locate an angel on earth if they didn't want to be found.

Belial took particular pride in locating the human lovers and relished in killing these angels even more than torturing humans.

Unfortunately for Belial, there were only a couple of ways he could find one to destroy.

The first method, and the one he took the greatest pleasure in planning, was to put the most innocent of humans in mortal danger. His favorite scenario involved having Mal park on the side of some street and wait for a young child or old lady to cross. If the hit and run went the way Belial wanted, an angel would try to save the person and he would make his move to capture it. However, this plan only worked if the particular human had an angel assigned to them. If they did not, Belial would not get to torture and kill a brother, but at least there would be one less human in this world. A win-win no matter how Belial looked at it.

The only other way to catch an angel involved direct association with the meat-bags.

Over the years, thousands of dollars had been paid by the unloved to all kinds of junkies, hookers, and miscreants for any tips regarding strange or abnormal activity, and specifically, any talk of miracles.

Just this evening, a piece of shit with a hundred dollar a day habit told him about a miracle he had seen with his very own eyes.

"So, so this guy, a regular guy, comes walking out of The Wrong Number on Avenue T and W. Sixth St., a couple of sheets to the wind and not paying attention to a fucking thing. All of a sudden, this delivery van comes around the corner doing fifty and heads straight for this schmuck. Before I can blink, this other guy comes out of nowhere—"

"What does he look like?" Belial interrupted, growing bored of this bag of bones.

"So, I'm getting to that."

"Get quicker," Belial sneered.

John started sweating even more. He hated these miserable fuckers with their five thousand dollar Armani suits, ten thousand dollar Rolexes and holier than thou attitudes.

He had to admit, though, when he was walking on his ass, without a dime in his pocket to get high, they could be a real lifesaver.

"Just before the van was about to splatter this guy," John continued, twitching from the onset of withdrawal, "some other dude comes outta nowhere, pushes him out of the way, and takes the full brunt of the hit on himself."

"I'm not impressed. You can't be hurting that bad," Belial said, growing more annoyed with each breath this human took.

"But that's not the miracle, Be," John pleaded.

"So, he's lying there, practically pinned under the trailer, and I swear to God—"

"No need," Belial said and laughed.

"Huh? Uh, whatever. This guy is laying there and all of a sudden he sprouts some mother-fucking wings and pushes the truck off him and about ten feet away."

"Then what?" Belial asked, his interest finally piqued.

"Then what? Well, after I shook the piss out of my shoe, I ran as fast and as far from that fucked up scene as possible."

"So you have no idea what happened to the drunk asshole or the guy with wings?"

"Nah, not really. After seeing something like that, I needed to get high and get my head straight. What'dya think?" John asked, looking at Belial, his desperation blatantly obvious. "Story should be good for a fifty or a hundred?"

Belial laughed again, his smile full of malice and his eyes shining with evil intent. From his

brushed leather wallet, he withdrew two brand new hundred-dollar bills.

"Here," Belial said, tossing the money on the floor. He laughed as John scurried like a rat going for the last piece of cheese and remembered a time, so long ago, when he had first seen a man on his knees after giving up his friend.

CHAPTER FOUR

The first time Joe had experienced what he called "angel essence euphoria" was sixteen years ago. He had been sixteen and went to the basement to smoke a joint. The basement was unfinished and used only by his mother to do laundry and his father when the old man and his friends needed a private place to discuss business.

The minute he entered, he remembered feeling like everything in his young life was glorious.

He immediately forgot all about his parents' bitter arguments over every little thing and the strange phone calls in the middle of the night that left his father sweating profusely and white as a sheet.

This sense of euphoria was better than the free feel of Mary Ann Maniscalco's ample right tit. It was better than the first time he had copped his father's car keys and took everyone for a ride in the Caddy. It was even better than the sensation he got whenever he had the house to himself and a copy of his mom's Cosmo in one hand and his pecker in the other.

Then he saw him. Bound by iron chains to a large metal crucifix. Each of his arms had a single needle sticking out of it that led to two different IV bags. Each bag was filling up with a beautiful blue liquid the same color as the sky on a clear, crisp fall day. His eyes had been covered by a black blindfold and his mouth was gagged.

The prisoner was the most attractive person Joe had ever seen. His skin bore no blemishes, scars, or wrinkles. It was practically translucent. His silken hair was a color Joe had never seen before. More than just blond, each strand shone with its own special highlight. Even in complete darkness, he could tell this was not human. This creature was better than human.

As Joe walked further into the room, he saw huge white feathers lying underneath the captive.

Joe had never seen anything like them. Not even in comic books.

But who would do this? Why was this beautiful creature being held against his will and what did his father have to do with any of this stuff? His mind was plagued with these questions and a hundred more, but at that moment, Joe was too busy enjoying this newfound feeling of joy that, apparently, came from being in the presence of a real live angel.

CHAPTER FIVE

Nan was tired. More tired than usual. The fatigue was getting worse as the days wore on. Usually, she could blame her exhaustion on how hard she worked, her age, and the tremendous amount of responsibility she had on her head, but right now she wasn't so certain. Soon, despite having no health insurance and nothing left in the bank, she knew she would have to see a doctor.

Not that Joe gave a shit. She could be bleeding from every orifice in her body and he'd still want her to make him something to eat. Lately, she questioned why she had even married him.

They were only sixteen when they started dating. She had just moved to Brooklyn, specifically Ave. U, from a seventeen-story apartment building in the projects on the Lower East Side of Manhattan. Nan was still getting used to being able to walk to the store by herself and not worrying about being mugged in the elevator when she met him. She remembered being mesmerized by him. So handsome and strong, he oozed charisma. When he walked down the avenue it was as if he owned it. Everyone stopped to say hello, and with good reason.

Joe's Father was Nino DeFalco, capo of a small Gambino crew that ran Avenue U. When it came to wise guys, that part of her move was not all that different from where she'd grown up. At that time, the mob still controlled many New York City streets.

Nothing was sold or stolen and no one was strong-armed or even walked down the block unless Nino knew about it and said it was okay. And, God forbid he didn't get his cut of any action happening on those streets. Many a local tough guy had gone missing for lesser insults to Nino.

Nan still remembered the shock and terror she felt the first time she had witnessed Nino's anger.

Joe had taken her to the neighborhood's annual feast. She couldn't recall which saint was supposed to be the recipient of the funds garnered from the sale of sausage and pepper heroes, zeppolli's, and "Kiss me, I'm Italian" t-shirts, but it was a well-known fact to everyone who lived there that any money made during the feast went directly into the pockets of Nino DeFalco.

Every night during the week-long celebration, in the middle of the rides filled with screaming kids, rigged games of chance for dollar store prizes, and an adult's only casino in the basement of St. Simon and Jude's church, was a small patch of land the neighborhood people called "the square" where a make-shift stage would be set up and long forgotten Italian singers or old time comediennes would perform for the old ladies.

On this one particular night, a couple of neighborhood teens, who should have known better, started heckling some old guinea comic. Nothing crazy.

No name calling, just some screaming out of the punch lines before the comic had his chance to finish the joke.

Nan could still remember the icy look Nino gave the teens and the angry way he dispatched his men to bring the offenders to him.

After that, Nino walked into the schoolyard with the kids and no one knew what happened. It wasn't until the next day, when she saw one of the teens with a black eye, swollen lip, and walking on crutches, that she really understood what a scary man Joe's Father was.

But that was a long time ago in a neighborhood that no longer existed. After Giuliani broke the mob's back, all the social-clubs where the made guys would sit and play cards closed, leaving the people who lived there feeling afraid and vulnerable. That was definitely when the whites started moving out and a more mixed group of New Yorker's moved in. Nan and Joe were just a few of the less than a handful of people who had decided to stay.

When they found Nino in the trunk of a car on Bay Parkway with the back of his head blown off, and Nan's mother-in-law had to be placed in a nursing home, she and Joe kept the house, she got a job, and life went on.

Nan knew something had died in her husband when the old man was killed. Gone was his famous swagger and self-confidence along with any sense of who he once was or would ever be.

She also knew what it was like to live under the specter of the mob, never knowing if or when your brothers or father might get mixed up with the wrong people and disappear.

Most normal people watched movies like The Godfather and television shows like The Sopranos and thought the life they portrayed was glamorous and exciting. They never saw the real damage it could do to a family.

But Nan knew it all too well. Her own father had gone to jail several times for bank robbery and would wind up spending three to four years at a time in the can, hanging out with people like Joe's old man.

And when her oldest brother, trying to emulate these men he saw every day in their flashy suits and expensive cars, tried to live the same way, he quickly wound up on the wrong side of the law and eventually made a deal with the Feds to turn state's evidence in return for his freedom.

She never saw him after that, and perhaps it was for the better. Joe knew about her brother, and despite who his father was, never let it come between them.

Struggling to get out of her 1992 piece of shit Cadillac Seville, another reminder of a past that no longer existed, Nan wondered where Joe was now. In her heart, she already knew—in that fucking basement, alone or with John, getting high and forgetting she was alive.

CHAPTER SIX

An angel had been here.

After an eternity spent fighting with and against each other, there was no mistaking the signs.

The angel's fragrance, like fresh cut grass and the particular blue of his essence—what the souls would have called blood—were all telltale clues of a heavenly presence on earth. The amount of the essence also told Michael that whoever it was, he was badly hurt and wouldn't have made it far. At least, not by himself.

But the one distinguishing factor all angels possessed that made them different from each other was their feathers. Based on the feathers left at the scene of the accident, Michael knew which angel he was looking for—Azriel.

Long and luxurious, Azriel's feathers were soft as snow and almost the same color. Only a pale shade of gray that laced the tips broke up the brilliance and purity of Azriel's white wings.

Whatever had happened to his friend, Michael knew from these remnants left behind it had been bad, but not the end.

He could tell immediately when one of his own returned to the void of non-existence. From the moment an angel was destroyed, he could feel an emptiness deep inside as if he had lost a small part of himself. And, in many ways, this was true.

Before men existed, before there was ever a planet earth, and way before the fall, their numbers had been beyond any human form of counting. And since there was no individuality among angels, there was never any need to count.

When one angel grew bored of angelic life or wanted to know what more existed beyond their immediate knowledge, they were quickly drowned out by the voices of the many still loyal to God and there was never any further discussion.

It was only when those angels who wanted more control over their own existence began interacting with humans that a war was waged and battle lines were drawn.

Though time had no meaning where he came from, it seemed to last forever.

It would still be going on if the unloved had not directly interfered with a human, causing his destiny to be completely altered.

Once that happened, God put Earth off limits to all angels unless commanded otherwise. He forbid them from mingling with souls—as angels referred to humans—and cast out any angels that broke this rule. In addition, he took away their wings and forever banished them to the place that they had once been so curious about, to live forever without their heavenly powers or the ability to hear his voice or feel his love again. The fallen would never experience euphoria and their own angelic essence would be stripped away, leaving them forever incomplete, empty, and unloved.

Only those angels ordered by God to deliver a message to a true believer, protect a special soul till their purpose in life was carried out or, as Michael noticed more and more, to find an unloved who was doing great harm and destruction on earth, would be allowed on the planet.

Sixteen years ago, Simon had been sent to do just that and never returned. So had Castiel and Michael didn't know why Azriel had been sent here but he knew this would not end the same way and was as certain of this as he was that an "unloved" had turned the corner and was looking right at him.

"Hello, Michael. Funny seeing you here."

CHAPTER SEVEN

Sixteen years ago

Nino DeFalco's biggest mistake was trusting Belial and his pack of wild dogs in the first place.

Sure, they had worked together in the past, and when it came to finding new girls for the whorehouses or getting the best deal on a few pounds of heroin, no one was better than that creepy fuck.

And, when Nino needed a specific piece of work done—one that couldn't be traced back to the DeFalco crew—Belial always made sure it got done and did it for a remarkably low price, as if Belial and his men enjoyed the work. He found out later they really did.

When the news came out that they found a couple of the NYPD's finest—who had worked for Nino for over ten years—dead in Bay Ridge, Nino thought, Good, they got it done.

But those poor fuckers had been skinned alive and then set on fire one limb at a time. That was gruesome and unnecessary to even a stone-cold killer like Nino.

Recently, Belial had come to him with the idea of kidnapping some guy and draining his blood a little at a time. And he'd expected him to believe the fucked up reason he'd given as to why they should.

"He's a fucking what?" Nino exclaimed, choking on his salami and provolone hero.

As always, when he got too close, the smell of burnt flesh radiated off Belial, assaulting Nino's nose and making his eyes water. The cheap aftershave he used to try and cover the smell was even worse. When he touched him, Nino felt an uncomfortable pain in his chest and chills down his spine but his choking stopped immediately.

"An angel," Belial answered.

"Are you serious? What the fuck is the matter with you? What are you, one of Jerry's kids?" Nino asked, referencing Jerry Lewis's poster children from the Muscular Dystrophy Association.

"Listen, Belial, I know you're a little different. I get that you never wear a coat, even when it's thirty degrees outside, and that I've never seen you eat or drink, but when you start talking about angels, I think maybe you're a little oobatz.

Belial smiled and started threading a silver coin, back and forth, through his fingers.

"I don't eat or drink because I find your food distasteful and without flavor. As for being different," Belial sneered, "I think you presume too much. Whether you believe me matters not." Belial looked directly into Nino's eyes as he went on. "It is what we can do for each other that makes our relationship necessary and mutually beneficial."

Nino stared right back into Belial's cold, dead eyes, even though it became increasingly difficult to maintain his gaze.

"Hey, Belial," Nino began, breaking the eye contact, "let me know if you've heard this one before. There were three guys that died. A black guy, a white guy, and a Spanish guy. As they're standing in front of the pearly gates, Gabriel says, 'Before you can come in, you each have to answer one question'. They all said okay and then the angel asks the white guy to spell dog. The white guy says, 'D.O.G.' 'Alright', Gabriel says, 'you can come in'. Then he asked the Spanish guy to spell cat. 'C.A.T.', the Spanish guy answers. 'Okay, you can come in,' Gabriel says. Then the angel says to the black guy, 'Spell Czechoslovakia.'"

Belial had no reaction but Nino's men were laughing hysterically.

"Guess you heard it before," Nino said, laughing, too. "So tell me again about this angel and what it has to do with me, and let's go over my part of this deal one more time."

Belial smiled an evil smile and told Nino DeFalco all about his new proposition. As he did so, without glancing once at his left hand, he continued to thread the coin.

CHAPTER EIGHT

"Joe...Joe...Joe...you down there?"

Was that Nan calling him? It sounded so far away, as if he was swimming at Coney and she was calling him back to the sand.

Joe could practically smell the beach. A combination of cotton-candy, spilled beer, and Nathan's Famous. In addition to Nan calling his name, Joe also heard the distinct cry of ice cold beer here.

The images varied as well. Nan in her black one-piece, her round bottom covered by a floral wrap to hide the thighs she considered too fat and the ones that he wanted to spend the rest of his life between. The warm gray water of the Atlantic ocean where Joe learned early on to keep away from spots where he felt sudden increases in water temperature, seemed to go on forever. Children and adults peed in the ocean all the time. In truth, it was honestly easier just to let it go into the sea than walking through the hot sand trying not to kick any on someone else's blanket or waiting on long lines at filthy public toilets.

"Joe..." It was Nan again. She was getting angry. The sounds of the shore grew less as her voice became louder, closer.

His wife had reached the last rung of the basement stairs before Joe forced himself to wake up from the drug-induced daydream he was enjoying.

He quickly jumped off the battered brown sofa and ran to stand in front of her.

"Hey, Baby, what're you doing down here?" Joe asked, avoiding his wife's eyes at all costs. "Baby my ass," she spat. She moved past him, a loaded hamper full of laundry in her arms, and headed straight for the back room where the washer and dryer were kept. Only today, the appliances had company—an angel.

Joe stepped in front of her. "Here, give me that. I'll do it."

Nan held tight to the hamper and pulled away. "Okay, how much did you spend this time?" she asked.

"What?" Joe asked, his head still spinning from the drugs in his system.

"You heard me. How much did you spend?" Her voice was tinged with sadness and exhaustion. "I'm so tired of this shit. You spend all day down here getting high and not only do I have to work to keep the lights on and food in our mouths, but I have to come home to more work while you use any extra money on that shit."

Joe stared at his feet like a child being scolded. This was not the first time they'd had this fight, and what made matters worse was she was right. She was always right.

"Listen to me, Nan," he said, his eyes still on the floor. "I've got something coming up, something that's gonna change our lives. In a little while, you'll never have to work again and all our problems will be over. I swear."

"What the fuck are you talking about?" The sound of her voice became shrill and angrier as she continued. "You're a junkie, Joe, and you'll always be a junkie. You can't work because you can't stop getting high. You spend all day and most of the night down here, spaced-out on God knows what and you don't take a shit without John at your side."

Nan turned around because she swore she'd never again let him see her cry.

"I'm tired." She struggled to go on. "So fucking tired. Of work, this house, and of you. I can't keep doing this."

Turning his wife around to face him, Joe pleaded. "Just give me one more chance, just one."

The tears on her face made his stomach turn. He knew he was the cause of all her misery and couldn't stand it. Lifting her face with all the gentleness he could muster, he looked her square in the eyes.

"I'll fix this. I'll clean up. I'll make things like they were when we were kids without a care in the world."

Her face showed no emotion but her eyes betrayed the cold, disbelieving attitude she struggled to hide. "Sure, Joe, whatever you say."

With that, the woman he had loved since he was sixteen turned and walked back up the stairs, leaving the dirty clothes and her piece of shit husband behind.

"I will turn things around," he said to himself. "I can't lose, I've got the angels on my side."

CHAPTER NINE

Azriel didn't understand what the people outside his prison were arguing about. The intricacies of human emotion were new to him, and from what he had heard, nothing he desired to comprehend.

Where he came from, personal problems didn't exist. Being of one mind, the angels were blessed with the consistent, overwhelming warmth of God's benevolent love for them. Because they all received this blessing equally, there was never any jealousy, anger, or hurt feelings. At least not since the war had ended.

Time was another human concept that Azriel never fully grasped. For humans, it was the most important part of their lives on earth. They kept track of it, marked its progress, and mourned the loss of any amount. To a man, each and every one prayed to God for more time at some point in their lives.

Please God, give me more time to watch my children grow, or to spend with my wife, or to get my life in order were their only requests when their time on this earth was almost over.

Azriel considered his current situation. With his wings clipped, his eyes and mouth obscured, and getting weaker by the hour, Az knew his own existence would soon be at an end. Without any way to share his mind with others, he didn't stand a chance.

The sound of the machine withdrawing his essence was the only noise he could hear. In its own way, it was peaceful. The most peace he had experienced since coming to this orb.

Unlike so many of his brothers, he was not enthralled by the human race. In fact, he never found himself curious about any of God's other creations, and maybe that's why the council had chosen him.

After the war in heaven, the council was formed to make sure all of the Lord's greatest creations were carefully monitored. It was the council's job to assign different angels to earth whose various duties included making sure souls were not interfered with or harmed in any way, to keep an eye on all the outcast angels, and to provide individual protection to very special souls whose time on earth was crucial to God's plan.

If any angels on assignment did not report in regularly, the council demanded answers. The only exception to this rule was Michael. Michael had a perpetual God's Pass, meaning he could come and go on earth as he saw fit without reporting his whereabouts constantly.

Some time ago, a few angels went missing and no one knew what had happened. Michael was sent to find them and report back to the council. His report was never discussed among other angels.

Before Azriel left, he was told by the council to reach out to Michael and learn from him everything he needed to know about the souls.

He tried, he really did. But, Michael was always so hard to locate. He was the only one with the ability to block his thoughts from other angels, making him next to impossible to find. Besides, it was common knowledge among angels that Michael had changed. Except for a select few who had fought by his side during the war, his time with the humans had made him solemn and unapproachable.

The room grew darker as Azriel got weaker.

He was losing consciousness. Soon all that he knew would be gone. Azriel could accept that, accept anything, but the thought of never feeling God's love or hearing his voice again was a pain he wasn't certain he could bear.

CHAPTER TEN

"Where is he, Belial?" Michael said, turning slowly to face his lifelong adversary.

"Where is who?" Belial stood there, eons worth of evil staring into Michael's eyes.

"You know of whom I speak," Michael answered. "He was sent by the council and—"

Belial's body tensed at the word.

"Do not speak to me of the council. They have no more power over this meat factory than they do in heaven." His voice seethed with anger. "They tend a store that no longer has an owner, a garden that reaps nothing but waste. They watch over a home in such disrepair that even the landlord wants nothing to do with it. They count for nothing, and who they send here or what they want of this flea-infested planet means nothing to me. I am an expatriate who no longer has a home to return to, and those of you who continue the charade of believing these meat-bags are better than his first creations have nothing to do with me or the people who represent me."

Michael could feel the rustling of his own feathers beneath his coat. How easy it would be to rip this creature asunder and be done with it. However, at this moment, it would not help his friend who, from all the evidence, was in serious trouble.

"If I find out your behind this," Michael said, his voice rising to almost a painful level, "I will destroy you and all who serve you. I promise this. I have not forgotten what is owed." Michael turned to leave, feeling no imminent threat from Belial.

"Don't you remember, Michael?" Belial asked, his voice full of malice and ill intent. "You already gave your word to someone else. Someone who means more to you than any angel in existence. Be careful, now. You wouldn't want any of your secrets getting out."

Belial's laugh sliced through Michael sharper than any real blade had ever felt.

"My God," he whispered to himself. "He knows."

CHAPTER ELEVEN

On a grass-covered hill overlooking the small town of Rigby, N.Y., population 7,500, Maria carefully examined the tomatoes she had been nurturing all spring for any signs of corruption or unwanted infestations.

There was a time when her life was not always so carefree. The only child of parents who'd died way too soon, Maria found her strength in the church. In fact, when she was younger, she thought she had heard God's calling and became a novitiate with the Sisters of Mercy.

When she realized she didn't really have a calling but a tremendous love of the Lord, she had been disappointed but continued to value her faith.

She vividly recalled the day she first met Michael. Her dollar store alarm clock had failed to wake her up. She was running late for her job as an assistant actuary at Whole World Life Insurance in Manhattan, the third largest life insurance provider in the state, and the thirty-first in the country.

How ironic, the little girl who was terrified of death had grown into a woman, still afraid, but one who now predicted the probability of its certainty on a case-by-case basis. It wasn't the most glamorous job, but she wasn't the most glamorous young lady.

Wiping the shower steam off the small bathroom mirror, Maria took a look at the woman in front of her. She was petite, like her mother before her, with long, curly dark hair and almond shaped eyes the color of charcoal.

She never considered herself pretty. Her nose was too large and her lips too small, but she'd been told her whole life that she had a smile that could light up a room.

Grabbing her jacket, keys, and travel mug of Starbucks dark roast, Maria got in her 2010 Toyota Celica and hit the gas.

She hadn't gone half a mile down the hill that led to the Amtrak station and the 9:00 am train, when a deer appeared out of nowhere.

It all happened so fast, like a blur. She didn't remember the car rolling over three times, or being trapped by her seatbelt as the car burst into flames around her, or those glimpses of her life that most people tell you pass in front of your eyes before you die.

What she did remember, with unwavering clarity, was Michael's beautiful face when she finally woke up.

At first she thought she must still be asleep, or perhaps she was dead. She had never seen anyone so perfect and she swore—though Michael would later say it was a trick of the light—that he had a luminescence that surrounded him, causing him to appear almost ethereal.

"Who are you? Where am I?" Maria's voice was hoarse from non-use.

"You are safe, in your home and have been for quite some time."

His voice was calming and she felt an immediate peace wash over her.

"My name is Michael and I was there when you had your accident. You were pretty badly hurt," he said.

"But how did I get here?" she asked, interrupting him though she could have listened to him speak forever. "What happened and why aren't I in the hospital?"

Michael bent lower and closer to her face. His nearness made any pain she might have felt disappear. Warmth spread over her body and she longed to be held by him.

"I promise I will answer all your questions after you rest," he whispered. Maria wasn't sure, but his breath smelled like fresh baked bread the same as her mother used to make.

"Just go to sleep and I'll be here when you wake," Michael assured her. And he was. That day and every day for the past year and a half.

CHAPTER TWELVE

Sixteen years ago

Joe's growing need to be in the presence of the beautiful angel in the basement had become a real problem.

His dependence on the angel for his newfound feelings of happiness made it necessary for Joe to visit him every day, sometimes more than once. He had managed to make an extra copy of the key to the room and anxiously awaited for any opportunities to pay him a visit.

Sometimes, if his father decided to work from home or pretend to be a normal dad and take his family out for a day trip to Coney, Joe would feign an illness or make up a homework assignment that just had to be in the next day in order to stay home.

He hadn't yet learned the words to describe addiction or to understand the sweating and shaking his body would suffer from were a direct result of being out of the angel's presence for too long. He only knew that the feelings were getting worse.

Then Friday came. Excited as he was about a couple of days off from school, it could not compare to the thought of his father taking his mom to Atlantic City for the weekend and Joe having the whole house all to himself.

The all too common stirrings associated with being all alone with the angel had started before his parents even left.

Once he was certain they were gone, he double checked all the door locks and made sure all the chain locks were secure.

The thrill he felt as he walked down the basement stairs was as tangible as any other feeling he had ever experienced. Pain, pleasure, excitement, and absolute happiness were nothing compared to turning the key and entering the angel's room.

Only this time, something was wrong. Something was very wrong, and Joe knew what it was because he had seen it before.

After the angel had been in the basement for a few weeks, Joe decided to do some snooping and find out why he was here and what his father wanted with him.

This curiosity led Joe to his father's club on Avenue U. After all, that was the place his old man normally conducted business and the place, Joe assumed, where he would find the answers he desperately needed.

Using his father's keys, Joe walked in the club. He was immediately struck by the all too familiar happy tingling he felt whenever he was about to be around his angel. But this was different. The feeling was definitely there, but it was weaker, less potent.

When he went in the back room, he immediately realized why.

Strapped to a crucifix identical to the one in his basement was another majestic angel. This one was the color of ebony, or more accurately, had once been. Joe could only imagine how dark and rich his skin tone was before he was left hanging here with his blood forcibly being withdrawn for God only knew how long.

His eyes were covered like the one in his basement. There were no individual feathers on the ground but something horrifically worse. Laying at the creature's feet were his complete set of wings. They were the most beautiful shade of gray with hints of black at the tips. From the jagged edges where the wings attached to the back of the angel, Joe could tell they had been sawed off its body.

Again the same question that plagued Joe since the angel had entered his life began to resurface. Why?

Joe could not fathom the answer and made a split second decision. Rifling through his father's desk, he found the keys to the angel's restraints. After he had opened the last one, Joe removed the gag from the ebony creature's mouth and the blindfold from its eyes. What was underneath horrified him for years to come. Someone has taken the angel's eyes.

As he helped the angel to the back door, Joe wept. And though he hadn't really done so in a very long time, he prayed for these beautiful creatures and asked God to forgive him, and especially to forgive his father for what he had done.

When he was finished, he crossed himself and said, "In the name of the Father, the son, and the holy ghost."

"Amen," the angel said as he left the club.

Now, his own personal angel looked the same way. The natural luminescence that surrounded him was fading, growing dimmer with each passing day, and the feathers that lay haphazardly at his feet were even more plentiful and sickly looking. His luxurious blond highlighted hair was now bland and thinning. Joe didn't need a doctor's degree to tell the angel was dying.

But, what could he do? Joe had already let the angel in his father's office go, and he lived in a state of constant fear that his father would find out. He hadn't grown up the son of Nino DeFalco without knowing if you took from Nino, he'd pay you back in spades.

He could still see his friend Paulie's face last year during the feast. The beating his old man had given that poor kid just for making fun of some old fart was brutal and meant to send a clear message—don't fuck with me.

What would his father do to him for letting his captives go? He didn't know exactly what they used the angels for, but he knew his father made good money from their blood.

Joe could no longer bear to look upon the sad figure that had given him so much pleasure. Turning to leave the room, he heard a muffled cry. He couldn't make out what the angel was trying to say because of the gag over his mouth.

Joe pulled out the rag that prevented the creature from speaking and the blindfold that kept it from seeing. As it turned out, Joe would never understand what the angel wanted to say because someone had cut its tongue out. And, just like the angel in his father's club, they had taken his eyes .

Joe started to cry. Why did they do this? What did that poor thing ever do to deserve this mutilation. It was just so unnecessary.

There was only one thing left for Joe to do. He found the key to the angel's restraints and opened them.

After his wrists and feet were free, Joe removed the IV needles and helped him out the back door. Grabbing the spare set of car keys off the hook where they were kept, Joe loaded the angel in the back of his father's Lincoln and drove away.

After he left him in the only place he could think of that might help, Joe realized he'd never even said goodbye. In fact, he hadn't said anything. No apology or pleas for forgiveness. Nothing.

Two weeks later, Joe was still experiencing the symptoms of withdrawal. He had no idea the diarrhea, upset stomach, and sleepless nights he'd felt ever since he let the angel go were the direct result of its absence.

To get his mind off things, Joe thought it might be a good idea to take all his friends, and maybe that pretty new girl, Nan, to the beach, his treat. In order to do that he'd need his father's money.

As he approached the back door to his father's club, he heard his father's voice. He was not alone.

"So there were three nuns," his father said, telling a joke Joe had heard a thousand times and his men probably heard more times than that. "And they were instructed to wash every part of their body with holy water that had touched a man's penis," Nino continued. "The first nun goes to the fountain containing the holy water and washes her hand. The second nun goes to the holy water and washes her vagina. All of a sudden, the Mother Superior shows up and says, "Look out ladies, I've got to gargle."

Nino's laughter always made Joe smile. It was full and robust and exuded pure joy. Much like his anger when something riled him, it burst out of him whenever he said or heard something funny.

His men, as was required, also laughed. A little too much, thought Joe. But, just as quickly as it started the good mood ended. His Father's voice changed and Joe knew instantly he was angry.

"What do you mean you still haven't found them?" Nino DeFalco shouted. "It's been two fucking weeks and all I got to show for it is my dick in my hand. First, someone breaks into my damn club and lets that angel go, then the one in my own fucking basement disappears. Did you find out, God forbid, how it escaped?"

Johnny Mac's voice was barely audible but Joe recognized him immediately due to his stutter. "Na-na—not a word, boss. It's li-li—like he va-va—vanished into th-th—thin air."

"Listen to me, you retarded fuck." Nino's voice was fill of venom. "Find them, find them now or I'll cut out your stupid fucking tongue and no one will ever have to listen to your ba-ba-ba—bullshit anymore."

Johnny Mac headed toward the back door but Joe had already run away.

The heat from the afternoon sun was like a gentle breeze on Joe's face compared to what his father would do to him when he found out what he'd done. But what choice did he have?

CHAPTER THIRTEEN

Sixteen years later

Joe hadn't been to his father's club in years. Not since the old man had died.

But he was getting antsy. It had been four hours since the last time he got high and waiting for the guy who would help him market the angel blood, as well as his own need to get off, was making it difficult to act calm and sit still.

All his life he had fidgeted. The drug addiction only made it that much worse.

This was the fourth time he had gotten-up, walked five feet towards the door, and then sat back down.

Sitting on the black leather chair, in front of his father's antique mahogany desk, Joe began tapping his fingers on the armrest.

His thoughts drifted to the last time he had waited in this very same room. Back then, this had been his father's office and the place where he conducted most of his business. In it, his father would take meetings with the members of his crew, accept his weekly tribute, and listen to various plans for the next big score.

Joe knew he was nothing like his old man. Most of the time he was glad of that fact. He knew Nino DeFalco had died for being who he was.

So far, he had gotten lucky with the heroin but he was smart enough to know that one wrong shot could take him out just as quickly as two in the back of the head.

Maybe with, literally, a little divine intervention, he might be able to straighten out his fucked up life, give Nan all she deserved, and with a little more luck, hold his head held high once again.

"We'll see," he mused, as the door opened. The smell of burnt flesh and crappy cologne was followed by Belial, along with his 6'6", 325-pound gorilla. He sat across from Joe and pulled a coin from his pocket.

"You wanted to see me, Joe?" Belial smirked. "Kid sick again? Maybe need a few bucks for the hospital bills?"

Every muscle in Joe's body tensed and he tightened his grip on the arms of the chair.

"Oh, that's right," Belial grinned, "little Joey never made it out of the hospital. St. Joseph's, wasn't it? What an amusing coincidence, dying in a hospital named after a saint who couldn't help your son with the same name. Fucking shame." He chuckled, threading his silver coin through his fingers.

"Oh well," Belial continued, as he nodded to his bodyguard who immediately handed him a $50 Cuban cigar. "If it's not your son, then maybe you need something for your wife. What's her name?"

"Nan," grunted the piece of meat as Belial smiled lasciviously.

Joe had heard enough. Nothing was worth this. Reaching into the pocket of his father's leather coat, Joe pulled out his old man's nine and aimed it between the side of meat's eyes.

"I ever hear you say her name again or even try to whisper it, I'll blow your fucking brains out."

With speed barely registered by the human eye, the living embodiment of brute strength grabbed Joe's wrist. A second later it broke. Joe went down like a load of shit, clutching his arm and screaming in agony. When he opened his eyes, the gun was gone and pointed at his head.

"Boys, boys. Let's just all calm down now," Belial said, looking more than satisfied at the turn of events. "Such violence," he continued, "is so unnecessary. Now Joe, Mal didn't mean anything and then you go aim a gun at his head. What did you expect would happen? You'd shoot him?" Belial snickered. "Here's a couple of hundred for your trouble. Use it for…whatever, and let's just say we forget the whole thing and you tell me what you really wanted." Belial threw the money on the desk.

Joe picked it up and gave it back to him.

"You know something, Belial?" His voice was shaky from pain. "You're right. Let's just forget everything. Shoulda known better than to threaten the big man. My fault, I guess. Just one thing, though. Something my old man used to say. 'If I've seen it once, I've seen it a thousand times. For every Goliath who thinks he's unbeatable, there's a David and his fucking rock.'

"What's that supposed to mean?" Belial asked, getting up to go.

"Nothing, nothing at all," Joe said. "You guys have a great day. Maybe I'll see you later." Joe watched them walk out. "Maybe I'll bring a sling-shot."

"Shut the door," Belial ordered as he got in the Lincoln. He was livid that Joe had dared mouth off to him, much less pulled a gun in his presence. Then to top it off with the insult of refusing his money? Who did this miserable piece of shit think he was? What he'd originally wanted was beside the point. In fact, he should have killed the little fucker when he'd offed his father sixteen years ago. Hindsight was twenty-twenty he supposed. He'd not given the kid a second thought back then because these shit-filled meat-bags were a dime a dozen and their puny lives meant less to him than the coin he played with. He was hoping now that attitude of indifference wasn't coming back to bite him in the ass.

"What do you think he wanted?" Mal asked, looking over the nine millimeter he had taken from Joe.

"How the fuck would I know. Put that thing away. We have larger problems to think about," Belial said. "Michael's looking for his missing soldier and I need to find him first."

CHAPTER FOURTEEN

Michael appeared behind the oak tree at the home he and Maria had shared for the past year. He tried not to apparate too often as the act of disappearing and reappearing, while convenient, came with the risk of being seen as you were doing it and prompted too many questions from mortals who liked their reality based on reality and not on heavenly intervention.

However, after speaking with Belial, he had an urgent need to see her now, right this second.

The woman he loved was in the garden tending to the vegetables. Her beautiful face put to rest any doubt over his actions to get here. After all, he would rather be banished from heaven forever and live for eternity on earth if it meant he could spend that time with Maria.

As he watched her, he couldn't help but notice the care with which she handled every plant. She tended her garden as his God had once tended his own. But, that was long ago when the Lord's attention was completely fixated on this spot in the universe. Now his gaze was concentrated elsewhere and his garden had sprung forth a multitude of weeds that threatened the life of all other beauty in this world.

As God's fiercest warrior, he knew he would do whatever was necessary to protect Maria. No matter what the cost to himself. For right now, she was fine, she was beautiful, and she was his.

He recalled the very first time he had seen her. He had gone into St. James Church briefly to get away from all the noise, filth, and people. He often went to churches to get a semblance of the peace and tranquility he used to feel before he came to this planet. It was the only place where he felt completely at home and closer to his Lord.

Maria had been sitting in the third pew from the front, making a rosary. Michael thought she was the most beautiful creature he had ever seen. There was a light in her eyes that reflected so much love and peace that was sadly missing from most humans. She intrigued him, and Michael found he couldn't look away.

After she was done, Michael made a split-second decision and followed her. He saw where she worked, and later, where she lived. From that day on, Michael made time every week to go to Maria's church and watch her pray. He wasn't certain what human love felt like, but he was positive that's exactly what he felt for her.

He had been following her, yet again, when she drove off the road to avoid the deer. In the blink of an eye, Michael threw away the rules he had lived his existence by and saved her life.

Whether it was right or wrong to do so never entered his thoughts. At that moment, the only thing that mattered was this woman he knew he could no longer live without. He had not regretted that decision since.

Michael approached her quietly, the most perfect red rose appearing in his right hand.

"Hello, beautiful," he said, holding out the rose. "I saw this and thought of you."

She turned, startled and confused by his sudden and silent arrival.

"How do you do that?" she asked, rising from her knees and accepting his gift.

"Do what?" he teased, smiling mischievously.

"Don't give me that. You know what," she replied, feigning annoyance.

"I just like to surprise you," Michael said, suddenly concerned that he had really upset the woman he adored. "I'm sorry," he apologized.

"C'mere, you!" She laughed, grabbing him by the lapels of his trench coat and kissing him softly and slowly.

Michael had known and experienced all the pleasure of paradise and still had never been happier than when he was in Maria's arms.

"I thought you were working today?"

"I finished early and I missed you," he answered, lost in her eyes and comforted by her touch.

"Well, Mr. big shot, it must be nice to be your own boss and not have to answer to anyone else about your comings and goings," she said, mocking him.

Michael had told Maria he was a private investigator for a large insurance company and his job was to watch people who made phony insurance claims for any sign of fraud. Not the truth, but not so different from his existence on earth that he couldn't make it believable. His job explained away frequent or long absences, and though he tried not to leave her very often, his work provided a cover when separation was absolutely necessary. Like recently.

"Hey," Maria said, requesting his attention, "remember me?"

"I could never forget you if I tried." He smiled and kissed her again.

As they walked arm and arm towards their home, Michael recalled a time, not so very long ago, when the only true happiness he'd ever known was almost taken away.

They were on their third date after her near fatal car accident.

He had taken her to see Book of Mormon on Broadway. While he detested crowds—anything could happen in a crowd—Maria loved the sights and sounds of the city and was more than passionate about live theater. So much so, she had told him, she owned practically every original cast recording of every Broadway musical that had opened in the last twenty years.

The irony of the choice of musical to see was not lost on Michael. He'd picked Book of Mormon because he found human interpretations of anything to do with God or the gospel to be fascinating. Even he had trouble trying to read the Bible and often thought to himself, if only they knew.

Afterwards, he had taken her to a restaurant where the walls were covered with caricatures of people he didn't know. Maria knew them all.

"Ooh look," she said, her voice growing higher with excitement. "That's Carol Channing, that one's Liza Minnelli. I love Liza. And there's Bernadette Peters." She stared at him for any sign of recognition, and seeing no acknowledgment, just continued. "I saw her play Mama Rose in a revival of Gypsy. I still get goosebumps when I think of her singing Mama's Turn.

He had no idea who she was talking about, but it didn't matter. She was happy and her eyes reflected great joy. She was enchanting and he loved her completely with no regrets.

Michael knew then and there he would take her to every musical in the world if her eyes would continue to shine as they did now.

He felt the other angel's presence long before he ever saw him at a nearby table.

It was Ezekiel. Preternaturally beautiful, as they all were, with long red hair the color of the setting sun.

Michael had never officially met him, but all angels knew their own kind and all angels knew God's warrior, Michael. The real question was, did Ezekiel see him?

Forced for eternity by the 'no interaction between angel and soul,' the rules were quite clear.

They could watch and they could intercede if a special soul was in mortal danger, but under no circumstances should they communicate or be part of the individual soul's life on earth.

Michael had clearly broken that rule when he fell in love with Maria. In fact, she probably should have died in that car accident but when Michael saw it occur, he just couldn't let it happen. Rules be damned. He knew he risked his unlimited "God's pass" and didn't care. Her life would be short in comparison to his eternity and he'd pay any price to spend that lifetime with her.

But, not now. He was not yet ready to answer the council's questions about her or about their relationship. At this moment, his main concern was formulating a plan to leave the restaurant without Ezekiel's notice.

Just then, the middle-aged man sitting across from Ezekiel began to choke on his food and clutch at his throat.

Ezekiel sat perfectly still, not moving at all. He made no effort to assist the human or ease his distress. Instantly, Michael knew why; his brother was not there to stop the man's death but to ensure it would happen as willed.

For some very special souls, those whose lives were nearing an end and who had lived a life of kindness and charity, the council sent an angel to make sure their transition from one plane to another would be easy and painless. Ezekiel was this man's guide on the rest of his journey.

Michael used this much-needed distraction to feign an illness, pay the check, and get Maria out of there.

As they grabbed their coats and left, Michael felt Ezekiel's gaze briefly shift his way. He never turned and never acknowledged the other angel. He also never knew if his secret was discovered.

Walking hand in hand back to Maria's car, he knew it didn't matter. He was with her now and he would keep her safe no matter what. Even if she wasn't his mission, Maria had become his existence and he wasn't giving her up without a fight.

The Toyota pulled away from the curb on 46th Street and 8th Avenue with neither occupant aware of the sinister gaze that had been trained on them since they left their home in Rigby.

Watching them leave, Malachi reached for his most beloved human invention, the cell phone, and called his boss.

"Yea, it's me," Mal said into the device. "Michael just left the city with his bag of meat. You want me to keep following?"

"No," Belial said, smiling on the other end of the call. "Let them have their time. Our time will come soon enough, and then Michael will fully understand the meaning of true loss."

CHAPTER FIFTEEN

Nan had been going up and down these same basement stairs ever since she and Joe began dating.

Back then, they would sneak downstairs for some serious make-out sessions and some hot and heavy petting. Her first sexual experience had been on that battered old brown couch with the guy she knew she would marry after their second date.

Now, it was just a sad reminder of the wasted years she had spent with her failed husband. A pitiful testament to a life that had little to no meaning.

It was as if she had let God down by existing in such a miserable way. And, she was certain, he had abandoned her for taking his precious gift for granted.

Nan had stopped praying altogether after they lost Joe Jr.

Alone in the hospital room, surrounded by loss and emptiness that threatened to consume her body and soul, she was certain her son's death was her fault.

In her head she knew it was impossible for her to have given Joey leukemia, but in her heart, broken and grieving for her only child, her guilt was all too real.

Flipping on the basement light, her thoughts drifted back to that old saying taught to every child in catechism,

"God helps those who help themselves." Those words rang as true today as the day she had lost him. Perhaps, she concluded as she mechanically sorted the colored clothes from the whites, if she had left Joe and taken the baby away from this nightmare, God would not have forsaken her and Joey would still be alive.

A noise resembling a muffled cry pulled her away from her own thoughts and back to the present.

She stood quiet until she heard it again. The sound was coming from the small room that housed the washer and dryer.

Turning around, Nan spotted Joe's iron bar covered in black electrical tape over in the corner.

Joe had called it his "better be good stick." He would take it with him whenever he felt threatened, like scoring in a bad neighborhood or if someone wanted to fuck with him.

She had thought it ridiculous but right at this moment was comforted by the weight of the weapon in her hand.

Silently, she approached the door to the small room and turned the knob. The iron bar fell from her grasp with a loud thud that Nan didn't even hear.

The very second she opened it Nan was engulfed by the most magnificent feelings of peace and calm, and a sense of euphoria she had never known before. Gone was the guilt, the self-doubt, the worry, and the pain that had plagued her for the past few months. As if in the midst of the best orgasm she had ever experienced, she quite loudly moaned, "Oh, God."

The feeling seemed to go on forever, and if truth be told, when that first wave finally did recede, the joy that remained was equally, if not more so, satisfying.

When at last she was a little more clearheaded, Nan opened her eyes and beheld the most beautiful creature she had ever seen. It would take another few minutes of staring before she got a grip on herself and really surveyed the situation.

Whatever it was she was certain, by the large wings protruding from its back, that it was not human.

"Oh sweet Jesus...God in heaven," she whispered when she noticed his eyes were covered, his mouth was gagged, and his limbs were bound. "Joe, what the hell have you done?"

CHAPTER SIXTEEN

John had walked up and down McDonald Avenue for the last half an hour. A product of the old neighborhood, he was as much a fixture on the streets of Avenue U as the corner pharmacy and the Carvel Ice Cream store.

In his thrift store jeans and second hand tee shirt, he was indistinguishable from anyone else except for the constant empty look of desperation that his eyes betrayed.

Pacing back and forth, he would occasionally break stride to acknowledge a familiar passerby with the requisite head bob.

His guts were beginning to tighten as the all too familiar unease of withdrawal began its assault on his central nervous system. Within the hour, he would start to sweat and shake uncontrollably.

John feared withdrawal, as most junkies do, more than the possibility of death from shooting bad shit or getting caught by the police.

After all, was there any better way to die than high off your ass and with a buzz on that made you forget your own mother?

He had been a junkie for most of his adult life, addicted to one drug or another. But, not always.

John Maleo was the youngest child of seven belonging to John Sr. and Sally Maleo. Rumor had it that the Maleo's were first cousins and that's why all their children were fucked up.

With large heads, small eyes, and more often than not, vacant looks, the children were Special Education students from the first grade up to the time they dropped out.

Ridiculed and constantly beat up, John found quick and certain refuge from the neighborhood bullies by getting so stoned he forgot everything and everyone else.

It wasn't until Joe DeFalco took pity on him and let him hang out at his house that his tormentors finally left him alone.

No one fucked with Joe. Not if you wanted to live. If you even looked at him wrong, there was always the chanced he'd tell his father and then you were really in trouble. Everyone on Avenue U knew Nino DeFalco and had heard all the stories about what he'd do if you messed with him or his.

Occasionally, they bore witness to his temper in the form of a lifeless corpse left in a trunk on Shore Parkway with the back of its head blown out.

Slower than most, even John knew he had scored big time when he landed Joe as a friend and "get high" partner.

"So, where the fuck is he?" John was getting desperate.

Sure, he could easily sneak into Joe's basement—learned how when he was eleven—but that angel juice never did have the same effect on him that most others seem to feel.

He remembered the first time he had tried angel essence. He wasn't impressed.

They had just found Nino dead and Joe was using anything he could get his hands on to get high and forget. New York was going through one of its drug crackdowns and dope was almost impossible to find. So, Joe found the next best thing.

Strung out and hurting, Joe had brought out a vial of clear blue liquid. He said it was angel's blood, and if you shot it, it was the most intense, the most climactic, the absolute best fucking high you would ever experience. The word angel didn't even register with John until later when Joe had told him all about the guy his father had kept in the basement. The only thing that mattered was the get high part.

In a pinch, John thought as he continued pacing, it might do. But his preference would always be heroin. The purer, the better.

John never noticed the black Lincoln Town car as it turned the corner and came to an abrupt stop in front of him.

"Get in the car."

Before he could even see the gorilla in the driver's seat, John recognized the sound of Mal's voice.

"Hey, Mal, what's up?" John said, his mind racing at the myriad ways he might have offended this walking wall. "Can't go anywhere right now…you understand."

The rear passenger window rolled down ever so slowly and stopped after a couple of inches. John knew what was coming and felt the first pangs of diarrhea cramps as he willed his ass cheeks closed.

"Get in the car. NOW!" Belial's voice was unmistakable, a mixture of snake venom and gravel.

Whatever this was, John knew it wasn't good. For a brief second he considered running, but who was he kidding. They were in a car and he could barely get his dope-sick body to respond to anything other than not soiling himself.

As if to punctuate his thought, Mal got out of the driver's seat and held the back door open for him.

By the time he got in the car, John was sweating profusely. Every piece of clothing he wore was drenched and sticking to his skin.

Silently he swore if God got him out of this, he'd never get high again.

"Be. What's good, what's going on?" John heard the fear in his voice and silently prayed harder to a deity he never truly believed in. "You kinda caught me at a bad time. I was right in the middle of doing a piece of work for Tommy Tottola," he lied, hoping it would make any difference, any at all. "You know Tommy. Runs Avenue X."

"Shut up," Belial spat as his fingers found his favorite coin.

"Hey, I didn't mean nothing," John stuttered, the smell of the cheap aftershave making him nauseous. "If you guys need me, I'll just finish up for Tommy and meet you back at your club."

"I said, shut up." John didn't even see the punch but he felt the excruciating pain as the cartilage in his nose crunched and the taste of his own blood appeared on his lips.

"I don't give a fuck who you were working for or what slimy junkie shit you thought you had to do," Belial said, using his silk handkerchief to wipe some of John's blood off his leather seat.

The Lincoln made an abrupt right turn, sending John head first into the door and spreading searing waves of pain throughout his entire skull.

"I want the angel," Belial demanded.

"Wha-I don't know nothing about no—"

The second blow was even harder and faster than the first. Instantly, John lost all control of his bowels and shit all over himself.

"Oh God—oh Jesus,", he prayed for all he was worth.

Belial's smile was inhuman. John had never see anything so malevolent in his entire life.

"Try again," Belial said, obviously amused. "I think you've reached a number that is no longer in service."

This time John's bladder released. Before he blacked out, he remembered how warm and soothing his own piss felt.

CHAPTER SEVENTEEN

The emergency room in Coney Island Hospital was packed as usual. A gunshot wound here, a stabbing there, and a very loud pregnant woman in labor in the cubicle adjacent to Joe's.

Her contractions were coming every four minutes and Joe knew this because each and every time she felt one, she would scream, "Motherfucker," at the top of her lungs.

"MOTHERFUCKER!"

Joe checked his watch. Right on cue.

His wrist hurt like that pregnant woman's favorite word but Joe's pride hurt even worse. Fucking Belial, he thought as he cradled his broken wrist. One of these days I'm going to put you in the ground, bury you and piss on your fucking grave.

His arm throbbed and Joe instinctively reached for the bottle of Percocet Nan's doctor had given her for back pain, the one that he had stolen weeks ago.

How many times had he fucked over his own wife. The number was endless.

"MOTHERFUCKER!"

His pregnant neighbor was right. He was a motherfucker when it came to Nan, and she deserved so much better.

The pills were hitting him nicely now and the familiar fog that enveloped him brought the added assistance of dulling his pain, as well as his memories.

Joe's eyes started the long slow blink followed by the customary junkie head nod. He was drifting away.

A gunshot rang out in the night. The blast had been muzzled by his father's silencer, but from the back of the ally, through a cracked slat in his father's boarded up club window, Joe could see and feel the impact of the bullet just as surely as Johnny Mac lying dead at his old man's feet, the single bullet hole in his forehead still smoking.

"I never liked that stuttering cock-sucker," his father calmly declared. "I know he had something to do with our missing feathered friends."

"But what about Belial?" Paulie G., Nino's right-hand man, asked nervously.

"What about him?" Nino replied, "I don't give a flying fuck about that creepy asshole."

Nino put the nine on the corner of his mahogany desk and took his seat.

"What're you going to tell him about another missing angel?" Paulie was methodically rolling Johnny Mac's body in the plastic tarp on which he was killed.

"I'm gonna tell him the truth," Nino declared. "Someone let him go and I took care of it."

"But what about the essence?"

"WHAT ABOUT IT?" Nino roared and jumped out of his chair. The speed of his father's movements startled Joe as his father picked up the nine and put it to Paulie's head.

Paulie stood perfectly still, and said, "Nothing, Nino. Nothing." His fear was so palpable, Joe's own breathing sped up, and he started sweating profusely.

"You're fucking right, nothing." Nino put the gun back in his pocket and moved towards his chair. He hadn't even realized he'd been standing on dead Johnny Mac's face.

"We should have never gotten into this angel blood bullshit. No matter how much money we made selling that blue shit to the junkies, it's just not worth it." Nino's voice was tinged with regret. "Fuck Belial, fuck his gorilla, fuck the money, and especially fuck angels." He picked up the picture of his wife and son that sat on his desk and stared at it.

"God help me," he whispered. "Belial, that MOTHERFUCKER!"

Why did his father suddenly sound like a woman? Joe's eyes sprang open and he was back in the E.R.

However, the image of Johnny Mac's face and the guilt he bore over his death lingered like a living, breathing nightmare.

The irony of his current situation wasn't lost on Joe. An innocent man had died because he let the angels go. Now he was keeping another one hostage and slowly draining it of its essence, just like his father.

"MOTHERFUCKER!"

That's what he was alright. But not for long. Soon all of his prayers would be answered and Nan could take it easy. They'd be okay and then he'd set the captive angel free.

I'm not my father, Joe tried to convince himself.

"MOTHERFUCKER!"

The how to do it was the problem. Joe popped another pill. His father had used Belial for the mechanics and marketing of the angels' essence. Joe remembered his old man used to say Belial knew all about these poor feathered fucks, so let him handle it.

"MOTHERFUCKER!"

Cradling his hurt wrist with his other arm, Joe knew the only thing he'd let Belial do now was die.

I'll figure it out myself, Joe thought. John will help me.

Joe started drifting again.

I'll get my shit tight once more and everything will be fine.

"MOTHERFUCKER!"

Joe smiled through the haze.

"You tell 'em, Sweetheart—you tell 'em. Motherfucker is right."

CHAPTER EIGHTEEN

Michael knew instantly who'd killed this poor soul in front of him.

The body had been sliced to pieces with a precision that insured the victim felt every cut but would not die until the sadistic murderer was ready for him to.

"Belial." Michael bent down to look for clues. "Only a monster would take such pleasure in tormenting a human. But why?"

Michael had left Maria sleeping and decided to take another look around the area where Azriel had disappeared. He was about to give up when he stumbled over the dead body.

Going through the dead man's pockets, Michael could not figure it out. Belial didn't even like being around the meat-bags, much less touching them himself. As much as he loved to watch them suffer and then die, he usually had Mal do his dirty work.

Michael recognized this soul from the neighborhood, though he didn't know him well.

From the needle tracks on what was left of his arms, Michael could tell he was a pretty bad drug abuser.

As long as he'd been on this world, he still could not understand the people. These souls, beloved by God more than any other creature, constantly searched for meaning in their lives using artificial means and chemical compounds when God's love was well within their grasp.

How many angels had fought and perished in the Great War over humans and their right to live their own lives blessed with God's gift of free will, unencumbered by any divine intervention.

Michael never knowingly questioned God, but looking at this poor dead soul laying on the ground he could only shake his head at the waste of this gift.

He pulled out an old, beat up business card from the dead man's back pocket. On the front was the name and address of a common neighborhood florist. Written on the back was an address Michael recognized almost immediately.

It was around the corner from this location where he had found Simon.

Michael's demeanor hardened as he recalled that rainy day more than fifteen years ago. Simon was the third angel to go missing in as many months.

The council had ordered Michael to find them and find out what happened to their shared mind connection.

The word on the street never mentioned angels, but it was becoming widely known that there was a powerful new drug making the rounds that gave the user an amazing euphoric feeling that lasted for as long as twenty-four hours. One shot cost $1,000 but once you experienced it, you'd kill your own mother for another taste.

Michael knew all about the powerful effect angel essence had on humans. Once a human felt that one of a kind euphoria, they would lose all reason and free will in order to sustain the feeling.

But some of the fallen, like Belial, considered humans nothing more than pets and enjoyed playing with their lives, no matter the cost.

The night Michael found Simon was cold and dark with thick cloud cover that impeded any light from the sky.

Michael had received a tip that this new drug could be purchased from a club on Avenue U in Brooklyn.

When he arrived at the nondescript storefront and looked around, he sensed an angel had been there. But it wasn't until he went into the back room that he was certain.

The walls were lined with wooden shelves that contained vial after vial of angel essence. If Simon still lived, he would be incredibly weak.

Searching for more clues, Michael was horrified by what he found next.

On the floor were Simon's once beautiful and majestic wings. They had been sawed off his back. Whoever committed this atrocity had been particularly cold and heartless.

An angel's wings, bestowed upon them by the creator, were their crowning jewel. Each set was different from all other angels' and treasured by them above all else, even though it was never discussed.

He could only imagine how his friend felt at having to witness his own desecration but quickly realized Simon couldn't have witnessed it. There, on a small table next to the metal crucifix where Simon had been restrained, were his brilliant blue-green eyes. With tears in his own eyes, Michael picked them up and placed them gently in his pocket. He wept for his friend and for the brutality he had been forced to endure.

Realizing that in his condition Simon couldn't have gotten far, Michael continued to search.

He followed the fresh trail of angel essence that led out the back door. Michael had walked only a few feet before he found his fallen friend.

"Simon!" Michael cried. Bending down, he took his fallen brother in his arms.

"I knew you'd come," Simon said, his voice barely above a whisper. "My wings—they cut off my wings."

"Who did this to you? Where are Castiel and Anakel?" Michael asked, trying in vain to comfort his friend but allowing his anger and need for vengeance to seep into his tone.

"I don't know. I could not see. They took my eyes."

Michael had forgotten about the eyes. "Do not worry. I have them," he said quietly. "It's okay, everything will be fine." Michael knew he was lying to both himself and Simon.

"They are strange creatures, these humans," Simon said, his breathing becoming shallow. "They have an immense capacity to love but are just as capable of unbelievable cruelty."

Michael looked at his friend's battered body. Where Simon's eyes should have been there were instead two gaping holes. All that was left of his incredible wings were jagged bone and featherless husks.

"Shh. Rest now." Michael held him tighter. "All will be well once more."

Then he kissed Simon goodbye, looked up to the sky, and asked the heavenly Father to forgive him for not arriving in time.

When he was finished, Michael looked back down. Simon was gone.

Who had done this? He had an idea but needed confirmation.

There was only one way to find out the answer. Reaching into his raincoat, Michael pulled out Simon's eyes. Holding them with love and care in the palm of his hand, Michael stared into them. Whoever hurt his brother did not know or didn't much care that an angel's eyes would continue to bear witness and record their surroundings whether attached to the angel or not.

His gaze never wavered as Michael watched everything that had happened to Simon. He watched as a five-year-old girl crossed the street with her grandmother and a car came straight for them. He watched as Simon pushed the souls out of the way and was hit by the car in their stead. Then he continued to watch as Malachi got out of the driver's seat of the car that hit Simon, took out a strange wooden dagger, and stabbed Simon in the side. He was immediately incapacitated and placed in the back seat of a black

Lincoln Town Car. This all happened in the blink of a human's eye and the little girl and old woman never knew a thing. But Michael saw it all, including the passenger in the back seat of the Lincoln—Belial.

After that, the eyes recorded Mal and Belial as they hooked Simon to the metal crucifix and started the task of draining his essence. The fallen smiled and laughed the entire time.

The rest of the time recorded was more of the same. Michael couldn't tell how long his brother had been tortured before the eyes bore witness to someone else.

The first human Simon's eyes showed was an older man that Michael recognized as a mid-level mobster that lived and worked in the same neighborhood where he had found Simon.

This man came in, pointed at Simon as he shook his head back and forth, and argued with Belial.

Without sound, Michael could not tell what they had said but the mobster looked almost sad as he walked out the door.

The last thing the eyes recorded before Michael found Simon was a teenage boy. He was obviously scared as he approached the angel and kept looking around the room. Then the young man in the black Yankee sweatshirt and Yankee baseball cap took out a key and unlocked Simon. There were tears in his eyes as he watched Simon struggle to leave, and he gave the sign of the cross before he himself left the building.

The eyes told Michael nothing about where he might find Castiel or Anakel, but now he knew for sure who was behind their disappearance. Based on the teenager's actions, he might not be too late to help them. He found out later he was wrong.

Two weeks after finding Simon's brutalized human form, Michael received another tip and found Anakel on the stairs of Our Lady of Grace church on Avenue X in Brooklyn. He was in the same condition as Simon, but as well as his eyes, his tongue had also been cut out rendering him speechless and unable to pray. Before he disappeared and in front of this manmade monument to the Lord, Michael prayed for them both.

Castiel was never found. He didn't have to be. Michael felt the loss of his missing friend as soon as he was gone. He didn't need to know how he was destroyed or by whom.

Now in the present, it was as if no time had passed and he had just lost them all over again. Michael looked at the dead human on the ground one last time before putting the old business card in his pocket. Sixteen years ago, he had been too late to help his friends or seek vengeance on Belial for the atrocities he'd committed.

Soon after Michael discovered the truth, Belial went into hiding, and try as he might, Michael could not find him.

However, he was back now and another angel, his brother Azriel, was missing. This time, Michael knew where to look. This time he would not be too late.

Leaving the dead junkie exactly as he found him, Michael offered up a silent prayer for his soul.

"Heavenly Father, please guide this poor soul on his path to your glory and grant him eternal peace at your side. Please strengthen me, Lord. Guide your servant's hand as I seek justice for all your heavenly creations. God, make strong my sword as I strike down the fallen and gut that piece of shit, Belial. In your name, I pray."

CHAPTER NINETEEN

"Where the fuck is John?" Joe wondered aloud, checking his phone for what seemed like the hundredth time. There were still the same six or seven calls as before, but no messages. Three of the calls had been from Nan but he'd have to call her back later. After he figured out what to do next with the angel.

The remaining calls were from a number he didn't recognize. The way Joe figured it, if it was important whoever it was would leave a message.

Joe was supposed to hook up with John hours ago but the hospital had taken forever to put a cast on his wrist and get him a prescription for 10 Tylenol with codeine.

"Not even Percocet," Joe grumbled to the nurse who had handed it to him. "Fucking doctors."

But John was nowhere to be found and that in and of itself was gnawing at the back of Joe's drug-addled mind. When it came to getting high or making money to get him high, John could be one patient son of a bitch.

"So, where is that jerk-off?"

As if in answer to his question, his cell phone, with David Bowie and Freddie Mercury singing Under Pressure as his ringtone, sounded. It was the same number that had called earlier.

Thinking it could be John using someone else's phone, Joe answered. "Hello?"

"Hey, Joe, what'dya know?"

Joe felt a chill run down his spine as he instantly recognized the voice on the other end. "What do you want, Belial? Why are you calling me?"

Joe had other questions like how'd you get my number and why don't you die, but wanted this phone call over as soon as possible. He instinctively reached for and retrieved a Marlboro from the inside pocket of his coat, found a book of matches in another pocket, and lit the cigarette, all using only one hand.

"Heard you were looking for John and thought maybe I could help you with that," Belial calmly stated.

Joe was getting worried. "Where is he, Belial? What did you do with him?"

"Why, Joe, you offend me. I simply had a chat with your friend. He was more than cooperative." Belial chuckled maliciously.

"If you fucked with him, I'll—" Joe began.

"You'll what? You live or die by my say-so you junkie piece of shit. Just keep your mouth shut and listen to me. Your father had the same fucking problem. Always running his mouth when he should have just listened. Maybe he'd still be alive if he shut the fuck up once in a while."

"What do you want?" Joe tried to sound hard, sound like his old man, but his hand was shaking so bad he could barely hold his cigarette.

"I want your winged friend," Belial said.

"Wha-I don't know what you're talking—" Joe searched for words, the panic evident in his voice.

"There you go again, Joe. Insulting my intelligence. Let me make this crystal fucking clear—you give me the angel and I leave you and your pretty little wife alone," Belial threatened. "Fuck with me," he laughed, "and I'll have Mal do a number on her while you watch until you both beg for the sweet release of death."

Joe lost his balance and fell to his knees.

"No," he pleaded into the phone.

"Now, here's what I need you to do."

Michael watched Joe fall from across the street. Blessed with preternatural hearing, he had heard Joe's end of the phone call and knew who had been on the other line.

Like father, like son, Michael thought.

After finding the old business card with the address to Joe's father's club on Avenue U in the dead junkie's pocket, Michael remembered where he had seen him before—with Joe DeFalco, Nino's son. In fact, as he recalled, they were always together. Or at least they used to be.

The phone conversation confirmed what Michael had already suspected. Joe was keeping Azriel, like his father before him, and Belial wanted him. That was not going to happen. Not this time.

Michael watched Joe get up on shaky legs and followed him around the corner to his home on Lake

Street and Avenue T. Hoping he would walk Azriel out or take him to his location, Michael waited.

After a minute or so, there was an anguished scream coming from inside Joe's house. Not wanting to disappear in front of any souls who might be wandering by, Michael ran as fast as possible across the street and into Joe's open house.

"No...no...no!" The cries seemed to be coming from the basement.

Michael ran down the stairs. Joe was sitting on the floor. In his broken right hand he held a letter and in the left a .45 automatic.

"She's gone," he said, not caring who had entered his home or what they wanted. "She said it was over, she couldn't live like this anymore."

"It will be okay, Joe," Michael said, carefully choosing his words and slowly moving closer to him.

Michael's voice was soothing and seemed to comfort the distraught man. After a few more seconds, he looked up from the letter.

"Who are you? What do you want?" Joe asked.

"My name is Michael and I'm here to help you."

Joe started to cry. It was obvious to Michael that he was overwhelmed.

"You can't help me. No one can. He's going to bury me and it's all my fault," Joe screamed, waving the gun haphazardly in the air.

"I won't let that happen, Joe," Michael swore. "Just tell me where Azriel is and we'll work all this out."

Michael inched closer to Joe.

"Azriel? Who the fuck is Azriel? I don't know no—wait, the angel? Is that his name? I never knew," Joe said, guilt washing over him and his thoughts drifting back to another time.

"Just tell me where he is." Michael's voice remained calm and steady as he moved even closer.

As if waking from a dream, Joe asked, "How do you know about any of this? What do you want with it?"

"I'll tell you everything," Michael said. "Just give me the gun and I'll answer all your questions. I promise."

"Huh? What? Joe began to speak but the ten Tylenol he had swallowed earlier were just hitting, making him speak and move as if in slow motion. Before he even remembered he had a gun, Michael grabbed his good arm and took the weapon away.

Joe got on his feet. "Give me back my fucking gun," Joe demanded, menace in his tone.

"Take it easy, Joe. Don't do anything rash." Michael said, attempting to calm the human down.

As if on cue, Joe did the exact opposite, and using all the strength he could muster, ran head first at Michael.

Joe's nose splattered the second it came into contact with Michael's knee. Michael never moved.

He could taste his own blood as it poured out of his nose and into his mouth. The warm metal taste made him sick to his stomach.

"I told you not to do anything rash. Now look at you," Michael said. Joe sat cross-legged on the floor, his good hand clutching his broken nose.

"Are you ready to listen to me or do you feel the need to break something else?" Michael asked. "Just tell me where Azriel is and I'll take care of Belial."

The mere mention of Belial's name made the pain from Joe's broken nose and wrist quadruple and sent his already sick stomach into spasms. In an attempt to prevent the vomit he now tasted in the back of his throat from rising any further and puking all over the place, he brought his head as close to the ground as possible. Without looking up, he offered Michael the letter he was still holding in his hand. Michael took it and began to read.

Joe, this letter is very hard for me to write, but probably one I should have written a long time ago. I'm leaving you, Joe, and I'm taking that poor creature you kept hidden in our basement. In our basement, Joe!

I've known for a while you were not the man I married but I never wanted to believe you could be capable of such cruelty. I loved you, Joe. Maybe a part of me always will but I can no longer live like this, and I shouldn't have to.

If you ever loved me, don't look for me. You won't find either one of us. I'm sorry I was never enough.

Nan

Joe couldn't stop it any longer and got sick where he sat. He needed to get off.

"Where would she go?" Michael asked, getting more annoyed as each second ticked by.

"What—I don't know," Joe answered, resignation beginning to sound in his voice. He was distracted by the thought of getting high and drifting away into the peace of forgetfulness.

"What difference does it make? She's gone and she's not coming back."

"Listen to me, you living piece of human garbage." Michael let his raincoat fall from his shoulders and his wings began to unfurl. "I couldn't care less about you or your personal problems." His voice, which had started at a normal timber, became as loud as a trumpet blast. "But I will not let Belial destroy another one of my own."

Joe sat in his own puke. Terrified, his whole body shook.

"You're going to get up, clean yourself off, and really concentrate on where she might have gone," Michael ordered, the soothing sound of his voice totally gone. "Then, you're going to take me to her and pray she's still with Azriel."

"She wouldn't hurt him," Joe said defeated in every way. "Nan wouldn't hurt a fly."

"It is not only Azriel I am worried about." Michael's voice became cold and hard. "I am worried for them both. If Belial finds them before we do—" Michael stopped speaking.

For the first time since he walked into the house and read Nan's letter, Joe was afraid, really afraid. And for the first time in a long time, he was not frightened for himself. He no longer cared what might happen to him but remembered Belial's phone call with vivid clarity, specifically what he said he would do to Nan. The more he thought about the sick malice in Belial's voice, the less afraid he became and the angrier he got.

Standing up, covered in his own blood and waste, he looked directly into Michael's startling blue eyes.

"Okay, Michael. Let's find your missing friend—and my wife. But listen to me and believe it. I don't care who or what the fuck you are—Belial is mine."

CHAPTER TWENTY

Nan drove down the interstate, her sister's Ford Taurus doing 65 mph. She felt unbelievably calm and clearheaded and wondered whether it was her newfound freedom that made her feel this way or her special passenger resting in the back seat.

"What the hell am I doing?" she asked herself for the hundredth time. She hadn't gone anywhere without Joe, except for work and food shopping, since before they started dating.

Nan put the electronic cigarette to her mouth and took a long pull. The mechanical substitute for good old tobacco had been her best friend for ten years, ever since she had that health scare with her heart. The doctors told her she should give up and that's what she did—to a point.

Joe, on the other hand, never gave up smoking and even when she was in the throes of a nicotine fit, would stand in front of her and puff away. That was Joe.

Nan glanced at the next green highway sign—Valhalla Exit 32B 4 miles.

"Valhalla—wasn't there something in Greek mythology about Valhalla being the place Gods went after they died?" She seemed to remember something like that.

The beautiful creature in the backseat began to stir. What would she do when he woke up?

His hair fell limp across his eyes. He was weak and had barely been able to make it to the car from the back door of the house. Nan's lower back still screamed from the effort it took to move him.

But, through it all, she had remained calm and serene.

When she started dancing in her seat, once again, she knew her bladder would no longer wait. Pulling into the very next rest stop, Nan parked as far away from prying eyes as she could get.

It would be difficult to explain the half-nude, unconscious man passed out in her back seat and she didn't want to try.

"Hey, pretty lady, what are you doing out here all by yourself?"

Nan turned to see who made the comment. Standing too close for comfort was one of the scariest men she had ever seen. He was tall, at least 6'3", and weighed a good 280 pounds. He wore a leather vest, the kind typically associated with biker gangs. His hair was dirty and unkempt with a scar across his face that extended from the corner of his left eye straight through to his mouth.

Instinctively, she clutched her purse tighter and silently cursed herself for not taking Joe's gun.

"I'm not alone." She tried to sound confident and assertive. "My husband is waiting in the car." Praying he would believe her and just go away, Nan turned around, walked towards the gas station, and left Mr. Scary where he stood.

Inside, where it was bright and there were other people around, she picked up a few essentials—toothpaste, toothbrush, soap, shampoo, a couple of pre-packaged ham and cheese sandwiches, and various pieces of chocolate candy—her favorite, and a must-have in every situation.

After she paid for the items with her debit card, she waited by the door a few minutes looking for any sign of Mr. Scary.

No motorcycle, no smell, and no discernible six-foot animals. Good, she thought to herself. Maybe he left.

Nan walked around back with the key she borrowed from the seventeen-year-old attendant who had been deeply engrossed in the latest trials and tribulations of Captain America. She smiled as she recalled all the old comic books—some of which were number ones—that she and Joe had sold on eBay. The money would go towards preparing a nursery and buy some much-needed supplies for the new baby. Those had been happy times. Where did they go? Gone like her dead son and failed marriage.

Perhaps it was the tears welling up in her eyes or her thoughts so far away that prevented her from seeing Mr. Scary until it was too late.

As soon as Nan turned the key in the bathroom lock, she felt the full force of his body against her own. Before she could scream, his hand was over her mouth. It smelled of grease and grime. and Nan couldn't breathe. She felt his spit on the back of her neck as he grunted, "You're all alone now, bitch."

With his hand still blocking her screams, he pushed her to the ground and began ripping at her clothes. Her head hit the ground with a sickening thud. It took all the effort she could muster to stay conscious.

As she felt herself slip away, the door burst open from the outside and she was temporarily blinded by the most brilliant light she had ever seen.

When her eyes had finally focused, Nan was shocked by what she saw. Standing above her and Mr. Scary was the most beautiful vision of perfection she could have ever imagined. There in front of her eyes was an angel, Joe's angel. No longer sickly and weak but strong and magnificent.

His wings filled the entire expanse of the bathroom. Their majesty took Nan's breath away.

With a speed that could never be measured, the angel grabbed her attacker by his throat and lifted the 280 lb. piece of shit off the floor.

"I will destroy you if she but asks it to be so." His voice was loud and fierce but induced a calming effect on her at the same time.

"No," she pleaded, "you can't."

"Why? He would not have spared you," the angel said, staring directly at Mr. Scary.

"I know, I know, but if he dies or mysteriously disappears, there will be a lot of questions that I can't answer."

"What shall we do with it then?" the angel asked.

Nan thought quickly. "I have some rope in the trunk. We'll tie this motherless fuck up and drop him a few miles down the road.

"Believe me," she continued, looking directly at Mr. Scary. "When and if someone finds him or he makes it back to the road, he'll have a hard time explaining how he tried to rape a woman at some rest stop, and an angel with wings stopped him."

Nan picked herself up off the ground, washed her face, and straightened her clothes. Her attacker, meanwhile, dangled two feet off the ground, securely trapped in the angel's steel grip.

Nancy DeFalco, previously Romano, had never been a pushover. Growing up in Brooklyn, you learned young to always be wary of strangers, watch your back at all times, and as the good sisters of Our Lady of Perpetual Hope had taught her over and over, 'Do unto others as you would have them do unto you.'

Truth be told, she always preferred Joe's version—'Do unto others and then split.' And with that thought, Nan grabbed Mr. Scary by his balls and squeezed until he passed out from the pain.

Not so scary now, she thought.

After disposing of the human garbage in a ditch a few miles down the road, Nan and her angel/protector sat in silence with only the radio playing her favorite classic rock station to mark the passing of time.

When Eric Clapton's Tears in Heaven was followed by Zeppelin's Stairway to Heaven, Nan got the message and figured it was time to say something.

"Thank you, for what you did back there."

"I am sorry he hurt you," the angel said, turning his head to look directly at her.

"I'll be okay. It'll take a lot more than some low-life, piece of gar—" Her voice started to break as the events of the whole day, and especially the past hour, came roaring to the forefront of her mind.

She began to weep.

"Please do not cry," he said, his voice like a salve that immediately dulled her pain. "The Lord will always love you."

"Huh...what? Oh, you're an angel—right," Nan said, making no effort to hide her disdain for true believer talk. "I'm sorry, it's just that God and I aren't really on speaking terms as of late. You get it, right?"

The angel looked as if he'd been struck.

"Guess not," Nan said.

"My Lord speaks to you, too?" he asked. "And you do not speak back?"

"It's not like that. I'm sorry—what's your name?" Nan was genuinely curious.

"I am called Azriel."

"Well, Azriel," Nan tried to explain, "God never really talked to me, and if he tried, I didn't hear him. When I said we're not on speaking terms, I just meant that I haven't prayed to the big guy in the sky for a very long time."

Azriel still looked hurt and confused. "Why not?

"It's not that easy to explain," she started, shifting uncomfortably in her seat. "A while ago, I needed something from him, something that meant more to me than my own life. So, I prayed to God for his help, and I don't think he was listening." The tears she had tried to hold back, once again started to flow. "Or maybe, he just didn't care."

"He heard you," Azriel said quietly.

"Then why didn't he answer me?"

"Perhaps he did and the answer was not what you wanted to hear," the angel said.

Nan was quiet and considered Azriel's answer. After a while, she reached down to lower the volume on the radio. The knob felt hard and real, reminding her that she was not dreaming and was really sitting in her car talking to a heavenly creature.

"What are you doing here?" she asked. "Don't you guys usually stay in heaven or aren't you supposed to be invisible or something?"

"I have been sent to Earth to watch over one of God's treasures," Azriel answered, turning away to look at the road. "I appear to you as I am now, because it is necessary. As you have correctly stated, usually our presence is unknown to humans."

"Treasure, huh?" Nan laughed at the absurdity of the situation. "Then how did you wind up with Joe? What did he want from you?" she asked, saving the question that had stayed with her ever since he rescued her from the bathroom for last. "Why didn't you stop him from hurting you?"

Azriel was silent for a long time. With his eyes shut, he seemed to be a million miles away.

When at last he spoke, there was a genuine sadness about him. "I have been sent to protect him and keep him safe."

"But why?" Nan asked. For the life of her, she could not fathom why someone like Joe would need heavenly protection, or for that matter, why he would be more worthy of divine intervention than her innocent child.

"I cannot tell you that, Mrs. DeFalco. I do not know," he answered.

"What do you mean, you don't know?" She was getting angry. "You're an angel sent from heaven—whatever that means. You're supposed to know everything. Aren't you?"

Nan started to shake. The weight of all that had happened combined with the number of questions that still had no answers threatened to crush her. She was hanging on to her sanity by a thin thread and wasn't sure how much more of this she could take. She reached in her purse and fumbled for her cigarette.

As she found it, she felt Azriel lightly touch her arm. Instantly, a sense of peace washed over her and she was, once again, calm and clear-headed.

"I am sorry you are troubled," he said. "It is not my intention to cause you distress."

Nan composed her thoughts before she went on. "It's not your fault. It's—it's a lot to process all at once. I mean, if you were watching out for Joe, why did he hurt you?"

"He did not know we were watching him," Azriel said. "I had to reveal myself to him the other day in order to save his life. When I woke up, I was bound and blindfolded and growing weaker by the hour. Then you found me."

"I'm sorry he did that to you," Nan apologized. "Joe can be mean as hell, but I've never known him to be intentionally cruel."

Azriel was sad again, as if he knew things she did not. "What happens now?" she asked.

"I will see you get to wherever you are going and then I must leave you." Azriel replied.

"What about Joe? What do I tell him?"

"Do not worry, Mrs. DeFalco," Azriel said and she believed him. "All will be made clear soon enough if you simply have faith."

Faith, Nan thought, was a luxury for people who hadn't lost a child or given their life away to a junkie. It would take a lot more than faith for Nan's life ever to be okay again.

CHAPTER TWENTY-ONE

Joe was getting sick again. His guts tightened with each minute that passed. The closeness of Michael was helping to slow some of his withdrawal symptoms but if he didn't get high soon, his body would rebel and he would be rendered fucking useless.

As it was, he could barely keep his eyes open and every time he thought he might sleep, the inability to get comfortable along with the constant leg cramps made rest a total and complete impossibility.

For what seemed like the hundredth time that hour, he wondered if Michael would give him a little of his blue essence, if only to get him straight. He considered asking, took another look at Michael's focused and determined face, and thought, Nah.

One thing was certain, this silence was not helping to take his mind off his jones.

"Where are we going?" Joe finally asked.

Michael never took his eyes off the road. "Upstate," he answered.

"Upstate? What are we going upstate for?" Joe's nerves were shot and his voice was becoming shrill.

"You tell me," Michael answered, starting to sound annoyed.

"How the fuck should I know." Joe was getting upset. "This is your party, remember. I'm only here for the ride."

"Azriel is getting stronger," Michael said. "I can see more images of his surroundings. I saw a sign that said Valhalla. What's in Valhalla?" he asked.

"There you go with the fucking questions again. You're the fucking miracle worker." Joe spat out the words. "And what do you mean you can see images of his surroundings? Can you see Nan? Is she with him?"

"We are not without some abilities here on earth," Michael said, his knuckles turning white from gripping the steering wheel tighter, his patience growing shorter with each passing moment. "As long as someone doesn't obscure our vision—" He stopped for a second to look at his traveling companion. "I can see where another angel is located."

"What about Nan?" Joe asked again. "Can you see her? Is she with him?"

"Yes, she is with him."

Joe let out a sigh of relief. "Handy tool as long as you don't like any privacy."

"Privacy is a human necessity," Michael lied. "Angels have no need of such human requirements."

"Hmm, so you guys never want some alone time?" Joe asked, giggling at the thought of taking a shit and having everyone else know how many turds you made.

The more he thought about it, the more Joe found this idea hysterical and started laughing until his drug deprived body rejected any semblance of happiness and his own need to use the toilet began to, literally, surface.

"Listen, dude," Joe said, turning to face Michael. "I've got to use the bathroom, like now."

"You will go when we stop," Michael replied.

"I don't think you get it, Angel-boy." Joe had had enough. "We've been driving for over two hours now and I really gotta go."

"You will wait," Michael repeated, his temper rising.

"I don't think you get it, Mikey," Joe replied. "I'm not asking. Pull the fuck over. NOW!" Michael swerved the car off the side of the road, causing Joe's head to hit the dashboard.

"GOD DAMN, SON OF A BITCH, MOTHER-FUCKING, COCK—" Before he could finish the word, Joe felt himself being lifted by the back of his neck and thrown head first out of the car.

Laying on the cold, hard ground, stunned and in pain, Joe couldn't decide what hurt worse—his head, his broken arm, or his broken nose. When he looked up, Michael was towering above him.

"Now you listen." Michael's voice was loud and commanding. "I know why you are ill. I have lived among your kind long enough to witness how you torture yourselves with fabrications of happiness. Whether it's pills or inhalants or needles, you all seek an end to your individual perceived pain when true peace can easily be found in all that God has given you."

Joe began to shake all over. His body wracked by spasms, his mind by shame, he started to cry for the man he once was and the human garbage he had become. A shadow of his former self, a man who kidnapped and tortured one of God's own creatures. He silently wished he still had his gun. He'd blow his brains out and be done with it all.

"I know," Michael said, "the euphoria you humans feel when you mix your own blood with ours. The temporary ecstasy that you seek above all else. Your kind knows nothing of true suffering. I have watched you live and die since your time began. I have witnessed how you teach your children to covet that which belongs to others, hate those who do not resemble yourselves, and how to kill in the name of he who is most holy. And, in the end, without fail, you all die screaming for his mercy."

Joe continued to cry. "I'm sorry. I'm so sorry," he said. "I never meant for any of this to happen. I only wanted to make things right and give Nan the kind of life she deserves. I'm sorry for what I did to your friend. I'm sorry for everything."

He raised his head to look at Michael. A soft light appeared to be emanating from the palms of his hands, bathing his entire form in a brilliant luminescence. Michael extended his hand to Joe and the moment they touched, Joe felt the most glorious tremor pass through his arm and slowly spread across his entire body. He had never felt anything like it. Not getting high, not shooting angel essence, not even getting laid.

It was as if he were bathing in a pool of warm water that reinvigorated every part of him, leaving Joe feeling whole and renewed.

And then, as quickly as it had started, it was over.

Joe hadn't even realized his eyes had been closed, but when he opened them, Michael had stopped glowing and was standing in front of him.

"What happened?" Joe asked, coming to the immediate realization that he was no longer sweaty, shaking, or in need of the bathroom. He couldn't quite remember the last time he was completely straight, his body totally clean of drugs, but he was certain this had been what it had felt like so many years ago.

"I have cleansed you of the poison that was corrupting your body, mind, and soul," Michael said, looking a little tired. "I have also healed the maladies that were causing you pain. Your life is your own, once again, to do with as you wish."

"But how—why?" Joe asked, wiping the dirt off his pants.

"There are gifts we have been given and things that we do that I am not at liberty to explain."

Michael started walking back towards the car. Grabbing the handle, he turned, once again, to face Joe. "I am still in need of your assistance. If we are to find your wife and Azriel before Belial, we must hurry. Will you help me?" Michael asked.

"Nan." The thought of his wife in trouble brought him back to the present. Suddenly, without any drugs to alter his thoughts and cause him to forget everything and everyone, Joe felt the full force of his love for his wife hit him like an oncoming train. He was clean and she didn't even know. For the first time in a long time, Joe had real, genuine hope.

"Absofuckinglutely, Mikey," Joe said, climbing out of the ditch with the ease and speed of a teenager. "Where are we going? Oh, yeah. Valhalla."

As he climbed in the passenger seat, Joe was struck by a long forgotten memory. "Hey, Mikey. I think I know where Nan and your buddy are going," he said.

"Good," Michael replied, turning the car keys and putting the Caddy into gear. "And my name is Michael."

CHAPTER TWENTY-TWO

The tracking device in Joe's car started transmitting again as soon as Michael and Joe were back on the road.

"Why do you think they stopped?" Mal asked Belial, who sat in the back of the Lincoln playing with his coin.

"How the fuck should I know?" Belial replied. "Maybe the meat-bag had to take a piss. Just don't lose them."

"I won't, Boss," Mal said as he continued to watch the road, glancing now and them at the tracker.

Belial was getting impatient. It had been far too long since he'd had a clear-cut way to hurt Michael, and Belial knew nothing hurt his former brother worse than torturing and killing one of his own. And once that was done, he would get rid of Michael for good and make sure that piece of shit Joe learned the real meaning of pain . But first, he would bleed Azriel dry and make a ton of money off his essence.

Not that he needed money. He had made more than he could ever use in an eternity by stringing out the meat-bags on angel essence and then making them earn for him in order to feed their habit for that precious blue liquid.

Belial turned his head to look out the window. It was the fall and the trees rushed by in a multi-color blur. How he hated this place, this garden, this world. And the longer he lived among these hideous souls, like gasoline added to a fire, the brighter his hatred burned.

He had been judged, found guilty, and sentenced to an eternity without grace by a Father who was supposed to love all his children. Never to hear his voice, feel that warmth or ever know the majestic glory of that love, was a price Belial had not been prepared to pay. He would mourn its loss till the end of time.

And, for what? he thought. What had been my unforgivable trespass that would cause me to suffer so?

Were angels not superior to men? Did they not deserve to be treated with respect and gratitude by those they were charged to safeguard? These were the questions that hounded Belial ever since he had killed a human who had offended him and was cast out of heaven.

"They should thank us for their very existence," he justified to himself, "yet they continue to mock us with their disbelief in all we know as truth and their ingratitude to a God who bestowed upon them the very right to make such choices." He despised them for their faithlessness, for their freedom, and especially for their souls—the biggest difference between angel and man.

Who are these ants that scurry about causing harm and pain to whomever and whatever crosses their paths to be given such a precious gift? What makes them so special and beloved by God? Belial would never understand, and this inability to explain God's choices or accept them made him bitter and full of hate.

Ever since Belial had been thrown out like so much refuge, he'd made it his sole purpose on this world to make the humans suffer for all he had lost. It made him less miserable and gave him something to do for eternity.

As he continued to glance out the window at a world that would never compare to the one that was taken from him, Belial spotted a human on the side of the road.

"Pull over, Mal," he said.

"Huh? What for?" Mal asked, as he quickly turned the steering wheel and came to a complete stop on the embankment.

"I'm bored," Belial said, an evil smirk upon his face. "I feel like some fun."

"What about Joe and Michael?"

"You said the tracking device is working fine," Belial replied as he lowered his tinted window. "We'll catch up to them soon enough."

Up ahead, walking very slowly and carefully, was a man in a leather vest and dirty jeans. To anyone else, he might have appeared imposing. To Belial, he was exactly what he needed to pass some time.

If he ever saw that bitch again, he'd have her begging for mercy and then kill her.

The same for that fucking freak that was with her. He would take particular pleasure in watching whatever that was suffer horribly.

The more he thought about it, the angrier he became.

Mr. Scary had spent most of his life angry. Angry at his father for what he did to him, angry at his mother for not giving a shit, and angry at the world for pretending he didn't exist. In return, he spent most of his life punishing others for his crappy childhood.

His junkie mother died when he was seven from an overdose and left young Mr. Scary with an abusive, alcoholic father who sold him to the highest bidder whenever he needed money for booze.

Struggling to climb out of the ditch that bitch and her friend had thrown him in, he remembered very clearly, the day he finally got his revenge.

He was fifteen and in 8th grade. Years behind others his age because of his home life. His father had been called to the school to talk to the principal. Usually he would not go, but this was serious and his father knew if social services got involved, they could take his son away along with his drinking money.

A couple of days earlier, young Mr. Scary had beat another boy senseless just because he could.

He'd broken three ribs and the poor kid's nose simply for the fact that he was an easy target whom everyone else labeled as gay.

For a while now, he had begun to question his own sexuality. The men he was sold to repulsed him, but deep down in his private thoughts, he found himself attracted to men more and more. He lived in terror that someone would find out about his secret feelings, especially his father, and God only knew what he would do to him after that.

The meeting had gone exactly like young Mr. Scary knew it would.

At 6'3", 280 lbs., his father was always imposing. But, put a few drinks under his belt and he was downright terrifying.

The principal, on the other hand, was 5'6", weighed 150 soaking wet, and had never hurt a fly.

"I imagine you know why I asked you to come in today, Mr. Lipnicki," his principal said.

"Don't imagine anything," young Mr. Scary's father growled, "just tell me what he did this time."

"He put another student in the hospital. He beat him so bad that—"

"What did the other boy do to him?" his father interrupted.

"Nothing, nothing at all. Your son has been calling him names and tormenting the boy for months."

"Why?" his father asked, not really interested in the answer.

"Maybe you should ask your son," the principal said, looking at young Mr. Scary.

"Hey, fuck-face, why did you beat this kid up?" His father's gaze was cold and intimidating.

"He's a fag. He made a pass at me," young Mr. Scary lied. "What was I supposed to do?"

"Well, there you go." His father turned to face the principal. "You heard him. This fag made a pass at him. He just put a stop to it. Case closed."

"I don't think you understand, Mr. Lipnicki." The principal had never met another man like this and never wanted to again. "We have no choice but to expel your son. Our school has a zero tolerance policy for any violence against another student."

"Why you lousy fucking—" Mr. Lipnicki reached out to grab the principal, but his son held him back.

"No, Pop, you can't," young Mr. Scary pleaded. "They'll put you in jail again."

"Get the fuck off me, you little piece of shit," his father yelled as he smacked him hard across the mouth.

Young Mr. Scary fell to the floor and hit his head. He would have blacked out if his rage hadn't taken over. Either way, what happened next was a blur that changed his whole life.

When his head was finally clear, his father lay on the ground, his brains bashed in by the fire extinguisher that lay on the floor next to him. The same one that that had been hanging above the principal's desk just a minute ago.

Once the cops arrived, they arrested him and brought young Mr. Scary to the nearest precinct.

He was charged with Manslaughter One and sentenced to five years in Greenhaven Correctional Facility, an adult-only prison.

Inside, he learned all sorts of new things. He learned how to knit because it passed the time between the rapes and beatings he endured. As a bonus, the knitting needles, once sharpened, made a badass weapon if the need arose.

He also learned how to speak Latin because no one understood the dead language and it made the white supremacists that protected him from other inmates, as he was passed from one to the other, laugh, as he called them every name in the book without their knowledge.

The last thing he learned was to make people suffer for all that he had suffered. Whether straight or gay, it didn't matter. Everyone was the same when they died by his hands.

Mr. Scary turned to see who'd pulled up behind him. His balls still ached from that bitch squeezing them with all her might, and his head felt like a hundred pound bowling ball that had been dropped one too many times, but basically all he really needed was to kick someone's ass and get back to his bike.

"Maybe," he considered, looking at the well-dressed guy stepping out of the back seat of the Lincoln Town Car, "I can kill two fags with one stone."

CHAPTER TWENTY-THREE

Belial had learned years ago how to tolerate the nearness of meat-bags. But no matter how long he lived among them, he never got used to that smell. A disgusting mix of sweat, shit, and desperation that assaulted his senses until he sent them away or killed them.

The guy in the vest with his facial scar, tattooed arms, and filthy hair was a prime example of human excrement. Under normal circumstances, Belial would have ended him quickly and painfully, but at this very moment, he was bored.

"So," Belial began, "what happened to your vehicle?"

Mr. Scary smiled at Belial as he tried to hide his disdain for the type of man he thought he was. "My bike gave out about a mile and a half down the road," he said. "I was trying to get to the nearest gas station when you guys were kind enough to stop."

"No problem," Belial said. "Always happy to help a fellow traveler. What is it you do for a living, Mr.— I'm sorry, I don't think I got your name."

"Herman. My name is Herman," Mr. Scary lied, trying to get a better look at the Lincoln's driver, who seemed like he might be a little more of a problem than the smelly asshole that sat next to him. Since he first sat down, the odor of cheap cologne was making his fucking eyes water.

"Well, Herman," Belial said, "what is it you do?"

Mr. Scary smiled. "Just about anything," he said, turning ever so slightly to face Belial directly.

"Really? Do tell," Belial said, getting way too much pleasure from his cat and mouse game.

"Do tell what?" Mr. Scary asked.

"Do tell me what 'just about anything' entails."

"Well," Mr. Scary said as he quickly reached out his hand and grabbed Belial by his windpipe and just as quickly pulled the hand back in agony.

His hand felt like it had been dipped in a vat of acid and looked the same way. The skin was hanging off his fingers and the bones were exposed. He had never felt this kind of pain. Not even when he crashed his bike and tore his knee to pieces.

He could barely hear himself scream over the pounding of his own heart. Mr. Scary was going into shock and starting to fall.

"Not so fast, meat-bag," Belial said, pulling a handy-wipe from his breast pocket that he wrapped around his hand and used to push Mr. Scary back into a seated position. "I'm not done with you yet."

Mr. Scary was moaning. His good right hand grasped the mangled remains of his left as he rocked back and forth.

"Are you listening, human—I mean Herman?" Belial asked menacingly.

"Jesus—Oh Jesus—Oh God," Mr. Scary repeated over and over, praying to names he knew but never believed in.

"That number's been disconnected," Belial said with an evil smile. "It's no longer in service."

"What the fuck did you do to me? Who the fuck are you?" Mr. Scary asked, struggling to get out each and every word.

"Much less than you deserve."

Belial pulled a hundred dollar Monte Cristo from his inside pocket. With the tip of his finger and a couple of puffs, the cigar glowed a bright red.

"Tell me a story," he said, as Mal snickered from the driver's seat. "If it's a good one, maybe I'll let you exit this car with some skin left on your body. If it bores me, well who knows what I'll burn next."

"What—what are you talking about? A story?" Mr. Scary asked, fresh tears welling in his eyes at the realization that he was going to die today.

"Tell me a story," Belial repeated. "Regale me with a tale of someone you made to suffer, someone you inflicted much pain on. You meat-bags are so good at hurting each other and I do love a good story. Just keep in mind, I bore easily."

Mr. Scary could barely think beyond the excruciating pain radiating throughout his arm, but he knew if he didn't come up with something, anything, this whatever this guy was would kill him on the spot.

"A few hours ago," Mr. Scary began, "I stopped to take a piss—"

"You humans and your bodily functions," Belial interrupted. "A disgusting piece of business if I do say so myself but please, do go on. Remember, it better be good."

Sweating from every pore in his body, Mr. Scary resumed the story he hoped would spare his life.

"When I came out of the john, I saw this great piece of ass. She was pretty for a middle-aged broad. She had real tits that didn't sag yet and an ass that was plump and juicy but not huge like all these young sluts are trying to get."

Mr. Scary stole a peek at Belial whose face showed no interest as he continued to smoke.

He went on, "My dick got hard right away, and I knew I was going to fuck her till she screamed for mercy."

"Go on." Belial said. "Tawdry tales tend to bore me but sadism and sodomy are two of my favorite subjects."

Mr. Scary swallowed hard as the sweat continued dripping down his face. "So I grabbed her from behind as she was going into the bathroom and put my hand over her mouth to cover her screams. She never had a chance. I ripped off her clothes with my other hand, fucked her brains out, and left her bleeding and crying on the floor."

When the story was over, Mr. Scary turned to look at his tormentor.

"Interesting," Belial said, the smoke from his cigar drifting up and out of the cracked windows of the car. "Too bad it's a damn lie."

"How— What do you mean, it's a lie?" Mr. Scary was starting to panic. "That's really what happened."

"Really?" Belial questioned as he placed the pinky finger of his right hand on the left side of Mr. Scary's face, watching as the skin instantly deteriorated, leaving nothing but teeth and gums underneath.

Mr. Scary's screams would have been heard for two miles if the Lincoln hadn't been soundproofed. Still clutching his mangled hand, he had no way to touch his face to determine how much damage had been done. But, when he could taste Belial's cigar smoke without opening his mouth, he knew it was horrendous.

"See," Belial said, "I've dealt with human garbage for more years than I wish to count and I've gotten really good at telling what's a lie and what's the truth. And you lied to me, Herman— you lied. Would you like to try that again or should I just touch every part of your body, starting with that useless piece of meat between your legs?"

"NO! NO! I'm sorry, so sorry, really," Mr. Scary begged. "I'll tell the truth, I swear."

"I hope so," Belial said. "I don't want to touch your dick as much as you don't want me to."

"No, I promise. I'll tell the truth," he pleaded as whatever spit he had left in his mouth came shooting out of the gaping hole in his face. "But, you may not believe me. I don't believe it. It happened, though. It really happened—honest."

"Tell me," Belial said. "I'll decide what I believe and what I don't."

Mr. Scary recounted every detail of his encounter with the woman and her otherworldly protector. He described his beautiful face, the light that seemed to emanate from him, and the grandeur of his unbelievable wings.

When he was done, he wept for himself and his miserable life.

"Did you hear that, Mal?" Belial asked the big man up front.

"Sure did, Boss," he replied.

"So Joe's bitch is with Azriel," Belial mused. "That's why Michael took Joe with him. Well now, that makes things more interesting."

"You-you know these people?" Mr. Scary asked.

Belial had momentarily forgotten the meat-bag was there. Looking at this pile of crap sitting next to him, Belial had an idea.

"Turn around, Mal," he ordered, totally disregarding the human's question.

"What about Michael?" Mal asked, changing lanes to get off on the very next exit.

"Michael and Azriel, and maybe if we're really lucky even Joe, will come to us," Belial said.

"How are you going to manage that?" Mal looked at Belial in the rear-view mirror, waiting for an answer.

"My new friend is going to help me," he said. "Aren't you, Herman"?

Mr. Scary felt himself losing consciousness. The last thing he remembered before he passed out was the sound of Belial's insidious laugh as he did his best to nod in agreement.

CHAPTER TWENTY-FOUR

Joe couldn't remember the last time he'd had a real dream. When he got high, he would just pass out after he'd had enough. If he had had any dreams, he definitely couldn't recall them.

But now that he was totally clean, he was having one helluva great dream.

He was in the basement of his house with Nan. Only, in the dream, it was no longer dark and depressing. The brick walls had been covered with sheetrock and painted a soothing shade of blue. Plush carpeting had replaced the hard gray concrete floor, and the beat-up old brown couch was now the most comfortable leather love seat he had ever felt.

They were talking like the old days. No yelling, no recriminations, and especially, no tears. He was making her laugh with one of his old jokes that she had heard a million times before.

As the dream continued, Nan asked him if he was happy. Joe put his hand on her lower belly and felt the warmth emanating from within. "More than happy," he said. "Ecstatic. What do you think we should name her?"

"Joe. Joe. JOE!"

The dream was over. Michael was shaking his arm and calling his name.

"Valhalla is the next exit," Michael said, both hands back on the steering wheel and fully focused on the road ahead. "Where do we go from there?"

"Keep to your left and at the second street light, make a right. Waterway Street is about three miles down. Once we get there, I'm sure I'll recognize Nan's old summer home. Her father practically built it from scratch and it's the only home in the area with a tire swing in the front yard."

"Good," Michael said, his face a mask of determination. "With any luck and Belial's own stupidity for planting a tracking device in your vehicle, he'll walk right into my trap and then I'll have him. I think it would be best if you waited across the street in the car and I will send Nan out to you."

"No way," Joe said, itching for his own fight with Belial. "I'm done hiding. When I was young, I hid behind my father's name and reputation. Then, when I got older, I hid from the world by forgetting there was one. Not anymore. Now it's my turn to be the man Nan has always deserved."

"Have it your way," Michael replied, "but know this—Belial will not be alone. Mal will be with him. I do not know how much strength was taken from Azriel, but on a good day, those two are more than a match for the both of us. Whatever you do, do not engage with either one of them. Get your wife out of there and head to the car.

Belial is more dangerous than you can ever imagine. Do you understand?" Michael asked.

"I understand," Joe heard himself say. But in his mind, he had already killed Belial in every conceivable way.

They sat in silence for a few minutes both lost in their own thoughts. "Can I ask you a question?" Joe finally said.

"What is it you wish to know?" Michael replied.

"What is heaven like?" Joe was having trouble believing those words had actually come out of his mouth, but after the life he'd led, he was genuinely curious and terrified of the answer, both at the same time.

"I cannot tell you that," Michael replied, a hint of sadness in his typically calm voice. "I have never been to your heaven."

"What do you mean, 'my heaven'?" Joe asked.

"Humans have a soul," Michael tried to explain. "When they die, their souls pass beyond a veil where angels cannot go."

"Then tell me what angel heaven is like." Joe really needed to know that any mistakes he had made in his past would be more than made up for when it came to the angels that had been a part of his life.

"Angels are immortal, Joe," Michael answered. "We can only perish when we are on earth in human form. Even then, there are only a few methods that can lead to our destruction. But once our existence is at an end, there is nothing more for us."

"That sucks," Joe said and meant it.

"No, not really," Michael said. "We live to love our lord and do his bidding. It is our greatest joy. Heaven, for angels, is the sound of his voice, the warmth of his love, and the purpose he had entrusted to us. We are his hands, his voice, and his message here on earth. It is all we ever need."

"Don't you ever get lonely?" Joe pressed.

Michael sighed. "It is difficult to explain to someone who can choose to be lonely or not," he said. "Angels are of one mind. We are given everything we will ever need or want by our holy Father. However, the longer we are among your kind, the harder it is to reject your individuality and the love you feel for one another. It is the primary reason we are not assigned to one person for their entire life. The temptations of your way of life can be overwhelming for one who is not used to it."

Michael grew silent. His thoughts drifted to Maria and his all-encompassing love for her. But, along with this love came the fears that had haunted him ever since they first met. He knew what they shared could not last.

She would grow old and he would never change. Eventually, he would have to tell her the truth or leave her alone. And, if he did tell her what he was, would she accept it? Could she love a creature so different from herself, a creature bound to God and one who had no soul?

Michael had these thoughts constantly. If she did accept him and they continued to share their lives with each other, how long would it be before they were found out and the council was told? He knew if that happened, there was a chance he would be cast-out, become an unloved, and although he would have Maria till her life was over, could he give up everything that had given his existence meaning? Could he give up his connection to all other angels, as well as the love he felt from his Lord?

On the other hand, if the council wanted, they could ban him from earth for eternity and he would never see her again. The very thought of this possibility filled him with terror. Either way, this was not the time or place to think about these things.

"I'm sorry if I offended you," Joe interrupted his thoughts.

"It is fine. You cannot offend me."

"Then can I ask you another question?" Joe said, gazing out the passenger window as the rows of homes filled with people living normal lives passed by.

"Yes," Michael replied, grateful for something else to think about.

"Why did Azriel save me?" Joe asked, not certain he wanted to know the answer or not.

"It is his mission to keep you safe and unharmed," Michael said.

"Why—why me?"

"There are things I cannot explain, matters that you would not understand," Michael answered.

"Like why I'm still here and my son is gone." Joe's eyes filled with tears as he remembered his beautiful child and how quickly he had been taken from them.

"Our heavenly Father does not tell us why some souls are called back to him after such a short time," Michael said, turning to face Joe. "What I can tell you is your son is with the Lord now and he is happy and free from any pain."

"You promise?" Joe asked, the tears he'd been trying to hide now freely flowing.

"I swear it."

"Alright then, let's get your friend and my wife and take care of Belial once and for all."

Joe pointed to a two-story home on the corner with a tire swing in the front and Nan's sister's car in the driveway.

"Let's do this," Joe said.

CHAPTER TWENTY-FIVE

Azriel was getting stronger. Very soon he would be able to leave Mrs. DeFalco and resume his heavenly duties.

They had arrived at her parents' summer home about an hour ago. She had gone into the kitchen to make a cup of coffee she said "she had to have or she would hurt someone."

Why would she do that? Azriel considered, completely unable of understanding human sarcasm.

The house was warm and inviting. The furniture was all over-sized and immensely comfortable with tons of throw pillows on every seat. In front of the fireplace, there was an antique oak rocking chair. On the mantel were dozens of picture frames of varying sizes, full of images of happy men, women, and children.

Azriel examined each and every one in hopes he might better understand human emotion, and more specifically, their love for one another.

He picked up a picture of Mrs. DeFalco beaming with joy at the infant she cradled in her arms.

"Please put that down." Nan had her cup of coffee in one hand and a plate of cookies in the other.

"I'm sorry," Azriel said. "I did not mean to upset you."

"You didn't, Azriel. That picture just makes me sad." Nan put her cup and the cookies she'd found in the pantry on the coffee table in front of the couch.

"Why?" Azriel asked, genuinely curious.

"I loved my son very much," Nan said, her voice breaking as she struggled to get out the words. "He passed away about a year after that picture was taken. He was the best thing in my life and now he's gone."

"I am sorry," Azriel said, placing the picture back in the same spot. "You still have your husband, though."

"My husband left me a long time ago, too," Nan said with a sigh.

"I do not understand. Do you not live together?" he asked.

"There are many different ways to leave a person," Nan tried to explain. "My husband made choices in his life that pushed me away and drove a wedge between us." Nan picked up their wedding picture and tried to remember being that young and carefree.

The day they were married was one of the happiest days of her life. Joe's father had been dead for a few years, and though his presence was fiercely missed, Joe had not yet let it consume his life, and the joy they both felt over getting married was as close to bliss as she could imagine.

Although they had already slept together many times, they both decided to stay apart the night before their wedding so when they saw each other the next day, it would be a surprise.

She had felt like a true princess in her $800 wedding gown, paid for on time, with tons of lace and a Victorian neckline. She did her own make-up—heavy on the blush because everyone said it would look better in the photographs—and had her hair professionally styled in the neighborhood shop she had used for years. She had dropped fifty pounds—again, for the camera—before the wedding but was still considered on the plump side. Joe always said, "A little extra cushion for the pushing," and at one time, she thought it was cute.

When she walked down the aisle of the church, his mother and a few of his friends on one side and her family on the other, she started to cry at how handsome he looked and how happy their lives would be.

Planning the ceremony, Father James had asked them if they had any particular bible verses they wanted him to use. Joe was out of his depth in this regard but Nan knew without hesitation which words she wanted to hear on her special day. It was Paul's letter to the Corinthians:

"If I speak in human and angelic tongues but do not have love, I am a resounding gong or a clashing cymbal. And if I have the gift of prophecy and comprehend all mysteries and all knowledge; if I have all faith so as to move mountains but do not have love, I am nothing. If I give away everything I own, and if I hand my body over so that I may boast but do not have love, I gain nothing.

Love is patient, love is kind. It is not jealous, love is not pompous, it is not inflated, it is not rude, it does not seek its own interests, it is not quick-tempered, it does not brood over injury, it does not rejoice over wrongdoing but rejoices with the truth. It bears all things, believes all things, hopes all things, endures all things.

Love never fails. If there are prophecies, they will be brought to nothing; if tongues, they will cease; if knowledge, it will be brought to nothing. For we know partially and we prophesy partially, but when the perfect comes, the partial will pass away. When I was a child, I used to talk as a child, think as a child, reason as a child; when I became a man, I put aside childish things. At present we see indistinctly, as in a mirror, but then face to face. At present I know partially; then I shall know fully, as I am fully known. So faith, hope, love remain, these three; but the greatest of these is love."

Nan had loved this verse ever since she was a child and read it in her weekly catechism class.

She couldn't think of any words more appropriate to describe how she felt that day.

The reception was a small affair in a mob owned establishment on 18th Avenue. They never even realized their wedding date was the same day as mother's day that year until the invites were already out. But the size didn't matter. Everyone who attended had said they had more fun at Joe and Nan's wedding than any they'd ever been to before.

Because their finances were so tight, they couldn't even pay the limo drivers and the hall until after they received their monetary gifts from their guests. That night, there would be no money for a honeymoon or fancy hotel suite so they spent their wedding night in a small no-tell motel on Bay Parkway.

It might not have been the most glamorous or expensive wedding anyone had ever seen, but the day culminated in their affirmation of love for one another that she was certain would last forever.

Still staring at the picture, Nan wished she could go back in time to that day when the only worry she had was the nagging feeling that no one got to be this happy. She was right.

Returning the frame to the mantel, Nan said softly, "I still love my husband very, very much, but I'm pretty sure we need to go our separate ways now."

"But why?" Azriel pressed.

"Because her husband is a piece of shit who treated the best thing in his life like absolute garbage."

Joe stood at the entrance to the living room. By his side was another stunning angel like Azriel.

"JOE! What—how?" Nan knew she was babbling but continued to struggle to find the right words. She was still incredibly mad at him, but at this very moment, could not remember why. The only thing she knew from the second she spotted him in this house, was how much she still loved her husband and how much she would always love him. It took her two whole seconds to run into his arms.

Joe held her for all he was worth. "I love you! I love you! I love you!" he repeated as he planted tiny kisses all over her face. "Please give me one more chance, just one more," he begged. "I promise this time I won't blow it. I promise for all that I'm worth!"

Nan took a good look at her husband and for the first time, in a long time, he was her husband and not some strung out junkie. His pupils weren't dilated and he wasn't slurring his words.

"How did you get well? What happened to the drugs?" she asked, holding his face in her hands and staring deeply into his eyes.

"I'll explain everything, I swear," Joe said, hugging her to him once again, "but first there's something I've got to do."

Joe reluctantly let his wife go and walked over to where Azriel stood by the mantel.

"I want to apologize for what I did to you. I'm so sorry. I never meant to hurt you." Joe looked directly into the angel's eyes, praying he could feel his sincerity. "I was sick and desperate," he glanced back at his wife, "and I never really thought about what I was doing to you. I never considered it might cause you pain. I'm so sorry. For everything."

Azriel was silent. He looked over at the photos on the mantel again and saw a picture of Nan, Joe, and their son. If happiness could be captured, it was evident in this snapshot of a better time for all of them. He might not understand human love yet, but now he had hope that one day he would.

"You are married to a wonderful woman," Azriel said.

"Thank you. I know that now." Joe smiled, his eyes fixated on Nan.

"Treat her as she deserves to be treated and we shall never speak of this again."

"I will," Joe said, "and thank you for saving my life. I know I can never repay you, but if there's ever anything you need from me, just ask."

"Make your wife happy again and that will be payment enough," Azriel said.

As if on cue, Michael walked towards Azriel until they stood face-to-face, no more than six inches apart.

"My brother," Michael said, taking Azriel in his arms and hugging him tight. "It is so good to see you."

"And you, as well," Azriel said, returning the hug.

When they had separated, they both knew words were no longer necessary. Being of one mind, they were already certain of how much they meant to each other.

"We must prepare," Michael began, his voice taking on its normal authoritative tone. "Belial and Malachi are on their way here. They mean to destroy me, kill the humans, and take you back to Brooklyn and completely drain you of your essence. This will not happen."

"Joe," Nan said, walking over to where her husband stood. She was noticeably scared. "What the hell is he talking about? Who the hell is this Belial and what does he want from us?"

Joe took his wife's hands in his own, where they belonged. "Don't worry about them, Nan. We got this. Michael and I—"

Before he could finish his sentence, Joe's cell phone rang. Looking down to see who it was, he turned and handed it to Michael.

With a voice that had lost the confidence it had possessed a moment ago, Joe said, "It's Belial."

CHAPTER TWENTY-SIX

Maria's neighbors, the McCormicks, had lived next door to her family since way before her parents died.

They had been married for fifty years, and as happens when a couple is together that long, they developed set patterns that they followed routinely every day.

Mr. McCormick was 89. He was a retired train conductor for the Manhattan Transit Association, whose 45 years on the job had left him almost completely deaf.

His wife, Eleanor, was a life-long housewife who had raised five children on one salary. To supplement their income, Mrs. McCormick would knit baby clothes and sell them at flea markets. With the extra money, she was able to get the kids a few things they really wanted.

But, that was quite a while ago. All her children were grown now with kids of their own and the only knitting she did was baby blankets for the newborns at Rigby's Children's Hospital. As long as she was still able, no baby would go home without their own blanket.

She was also a big fan of crossword puzzles—any crossword puzzles. When the kids came over to visit, they would bring her a bunch of crossword puzzle magazines.

On this day, Mr. McCormick was sitting in his usual spot on the recliner in front of the television. His hearing aid was turned down low and he preferred it this way. He didn't need to hear the old movies on the Turner Classic Movies channel, since he had seen them all so many times before. He, especially, didn't need to hear his wife scream for help with her puzzle every five minutes. Truth be told, he thought it was funny when she had to repeat herself over and over. Like she was doing now.

"Ed, I need a five letter word for terrifying," she asked without looking up.

"What?" he answered, starting to giggle.

"A five letter word for terrifying?" she asked again, getting annoyed as her voice grew louder.

"Huh?" he said with a smile. This would be good.

Screaming at the top of her lungs, she said, "A FIVE LETTER WORD FOR TERRIFYING!"

"Scary," the human wall with a hole in his face and a skeleton hand said as he grabbed Mrs. McCormick's puzzle magazine and shoved it down her throat until she could no longer catch a breath and died where she sat.

"Made you choke on your own words, bitch," he said, an evil grin on his face.

"Eleanor, did you come up with that word?" her husband asked, upset that his little game had ended so soon.

"Yeah, she got it," Mr. Scary said as he used Mrs. McCormick's knitting needle to stab Mr. McCormick in his jugular and watched as he bled out.

Whatever that creep in the Lincoln has shot him up with, he had to admit he was feeling no pain. and was actually getting a big kick from what he had accomplished here.

"Sic fiat," he said in Latin as he picked up Mrs. McCormick's knitting from the table and wiped off the blood from the needle he had used to kill her husband.

Let's see what we have here, he thought as he sat on a chair near the kitchen window where he started to knit as he waited for his next victim.

CHAPTER TWENTY-SEVEN

An hour later, Maria pulled into her driveway.

On any other day, she might have found the motorcycle parked in front of her neighbors' house a little strange. After all, the McCormicks were both in their eighties.

She might have also noticed the unmistakable odor of burning flesh, but Maria was in a hurry.

Michael would be home soon and she was going to make him her famous baked ziti and meatballs.

Her mother had been a fantastic cook and Maria learned by her side when she was very young.

Maria opened the door to the little house she shared with Michael. Despite his reluctance to talk about his past, she had never been happier.

She put the groceries on the kitchen counter, took off her jacket, and began looking for the right pots and pans for the ziti.

"Oh crap!" Maria jumped back. In her rush to get started, she dropped the glass lid for the saucepot and watched as it broke into pieces.

Bending down to pick-up the larger shards of glass, Maria carefully placed them on the countertop. Before she grabbed the broom and dustpan, she turned the music-streaming app on her cell phone to her favorite station, Broadway Hits. Nothing like some good music to keep you company while you cook.

As I Don't Know How to Love Him from Jesus Christ Superstar played, Maria swept up the remaining glass on the floor and threw it in the garbage can.

"He's a man. He's just a man and I've had so many men before in many, many ways—he's just one more," Maria sang at the top of her lungs, skipping and replacing words she didn't know.

"You have a very pretty voice."

Maria's stomach turned as she looked up from the can of spaghetti sauce she was opening.

Standing in her kitchen, no more than a foot away, was the most frightening image she had ever seen. It was a man. At least, she thought it was a man but it was hard to be certain. Half of his face had been badly disfigured with loose skin still hanging from a gaping hole in his cheek. His left eye drooped badly and was practically shut.

She tried to scream, but before a sound could come out he clamped his hand, or the bones of his hand since it no longer had any skin, over her mouth.

The smell of burnt human flesh and the feel of his peeling skin on her face made her gag and forced her to swallow the bile that lurched up her throat and into her mouth.

"We can do this the easy way or the hard way," Mr. Scary whispered in her ear as he pressed his hard on into her leg. "Either way, I'm good."

Barbra Streisand's beautiful rendition of Oh My Man from Funny Girl played in the background of Maria's worst nightmare and all she could think about was Michael. Will I ever see him again? Does he know how much I love him? She hoped so and prayed to God that he did.

"Now," Mr. Scary said as the excess spit spilled out of the hole in his face, "we're going to take a ride and meet up with some folks in Brooklyn."

"I'm going to let go of your mouth, but if you scream, if your voice rises above a volume I don't like, I'll fill your mouth with something so you can't make a sound." He smiled as his face continued to look as if it wanted to be anywhere else but on him.

Mr. Scary slowly let go of his grip. "Where are your garbage bag tie-wraps?" he asked.

"I—I don't use plastic, only paper," Maria stammered.

"Oh, for the love of— What the fuck is wrong with you fucking recycle people?" He was rambling as he looked through her kitchen drawers for something else he could use to restrain her.

Maria jumped on the opportunity. Before he knew what was happening, she quickly grabbed a large piece of glass still sitting on her counter-top and plunged it into her attacker's right eye.

Will you join in our crusade. Who will be strong and stand with me. Somewhere beyond the barricade is there a land you want to see ...

Maria ran for the front door as fast as she could. She opened it but was stopped by the chain lock Michael insisted she use for extra security.

When the beating of your heart matches the beating of the drum, there is a life about to start when tomorrow comes...

She fumbled with the chain and managed to unlock it.

Before she could open the door, Mr. Scary grabbed her by the arm and threw her to the ground.

The piece of glass was sticking out of his eye grotesquely, and blood dripped down his face and into the hole on the side of his mouth.

"I guess the hard way it is," he sneered as his mangled hand came crashing into her face.

Love...love is never gone, as we travel on, love's what we'll remember...

Maria loved that song from A Chorus Line. It played on her phone and in her head as her final thoughts before the curtain came down were of Michael.

CHAPTER TWENTY-EIGHT

Joe had never seen anyone crush a cell phone with their bare hand, but that's exactly what Michael did when he had finished talking to Belial.

"He has her," Michael said, mostly to himself as his knees gave out and he sank to the floor.

"What are you talking about, Michael?" Azriel asked, grabbing his brother by the arms. "He has who?"

"Maria—my Maria."

"Who's Maria?" Joe asked, standing next to his wife and grasping her hand a little tighter.

"Maria is the woman I love," he admitted for the first time in his existence. "She's all I care about."

"Michael, what are you saying?" Azriel asked, visibly wounded.

Michael buried his head in his hands. "You heard me. I love her and she loves me. We have been together for almost two human years. She encompasses everything that is good in your world. She is kind, generous, and only wishes to do good for her fellow man. I love her as much as our Father loves them all."

"More," Joe said, looking into his wife's eyes. "We cannot choose who we love or stop loving them because we're told it would be for the best." He gently squeezed

Nan's hand. "We only know we would die to make them happy, kill to keep them safe, and sometimes lie so they'll never, ever leave us."

"Yes," Michael said, looking up at Azriel for a glimmer of understanding. "That is exactly how I feel."

"But the rules," Azriel said. "The council—they will not understand. They will cast you out, or worse."

"They can try," Michael said as he got back on his feet, "but right now Belial has Maria and I have no doubt he will kill her to make me suffer. Just as he did so many times before."

"Then let's go make him suffer," Joe said, with a determination he hadn't felt in a long time. "I owe that cocksucker big-time for all the pain he has caused my family—and yours."

Michael gave a hint of a smile. "While I appreciate your willingness to help us and understand your need for vengeance all too well, I cannot ask you to help us. I must insist that you go home where you and your wife will be safe and out of harm's way."

"Maybe he's right, Joe," Nan interrupted before Joe could protest. Her face was soft and full of concern. "This world has just gotten infinitely larger for us in the span of only a few hours. I'm pretty sure we weren't meant to and aren't equipped to fight this fight."

Nan continued, holding her husband's head in her hands and staring into his eyes. "I know you want to help and I know why, but I think we should leave this battle to Michael and Azriel. I can't lose you again. Not again."

Joe looked at his wife, and at that moment, he knew he had his whole life back. He nodded in agreement and turned to address Michael. "Do you need anything—anything at all? I have some guns, untraceable, back in the house. Are you prepared?" he asked. "Where is this going down?"

Michael smiled at him. "You humans never cease to surprise me. As easy as it is for you to hate, your propensity for love is so much stronger. Thank you for reminding me of this. Azriel and I are to meet Belial in a few hours in Coney Island. Some place called the Hell-Hole. Do you know of it?" he asked Joe.

"Do I know of it?" Joe replied, amused at the question, "I practically lived there as a kid. I'll give you the address and draw a diagram showing all the exits and entrances. At the very least, you won't go in their blind."

"Thank you, again," Michael said and meant it. "I am sorry for the harsh things I said to you earlier. They were not true."

"Sure they were," Joe said and smiled. "They were all true. But, despite that, you gave me a second chance." Joe looked at Nan. "As long as I live," he went on, "I'll never be able to repay you for that."

"Oh, I wouldn't say that," Michael said, looking squarely at Azriel. "Your story is far from over."

CHAPTER TWENTY-NINE

Over two thousand years ago and half a world away from Valhalla, a man was killed who was so much more than a man. He was the living embodiment of God's love on earth—his only son.

On the day he died, the angels were busy. Each one was given a job to do to make sure nothing interfered with what had to happen.

Michael and Belial had been given the sad task of making sure God's son's crucifixion, and the events leading up to it, were carried out without any problems.

For Michael, it has been an excruciating experience. His love of God was so overwhelming, it was as if he could feel each nail as it pierced the Lord's flesh.

Belial did not feel the same way. He was annoyed to be around so many humans though he had to admit their pain gave him great pleasure.

He would never understand God's fascination with these creatures. In Belial's mind, his Father had already created perfection when he made the angels. He was certain, these humans were just an annoying way for the Lord to pass eternity. There was no way he could possibly care about them.

As for his son, Belial found the very thought of a mix between heavenly grace and human life to be an affront to every angel in existence. Just the idea that this human was considered the son of God made Belial furious and filled with anger. As far as he was concerned, the only true children God had were the angels. He found this whole assignment to be meaningless and beneath him.

On this particular day, he was ordered to keep watch over a human named Judas.

For Belial, Judas was a miserable little cretin who had been fated to give up God's impostor son to the Romans.

His job was to keep others from hurting him or keep him from hurting himself. But what fun was there in that?

Instead, after Jesus's death, when Belial could have prevented Judas from tying a rope around his neck and hanging himself, he chose to watch him die. As a souvenir, Belial took the silver coins Judas had been paid for his information about Christ and a branch of the tree he had died upon.

When Michael found out about his refusal to follow orders, he'd had a brutal fight with Belial. It had gone on for hours and when, at last, Michael was about to destroy him, God put an end to their battle. He was to exact his own vengeance on his rogue angel.

Not only did he strip Belial of his wings and ban him from heaven, to live for eternity without ever feeling his love or hearing his voice, he sent him to live among those creations that he despised the most.

In addition, because one angel's sins were considered the sins of all angels, God cursed the tree Judas used to kill himself and left it as the only weapon on earth that could kill an angel thus reminding one and all that no one was above the Lord.

CHAPTER THIRTY

Belial threaded the silver coin back and forth through the fingers of his left hand. In his right was the ragged remains of an angel feather covered in dried angel essence.

He couldn't remember the last time he had been this excited. Not since his fall so many millennia ago had he been so eager to engage his brothers in battle. Inflicting pain had become part and parcel of who he was, his very being. But the idea of destroying God's fiercest warrior and his constant opponent filled him with a pleasure that he hadn't felt in forever. This time the suffering would be special. This time Michael would suffer for all their sins, starting with his female's.

Belial looked over at Maria. She was tied to a wooden chair, her bloodied face a testament to how easy it was for humans to be brutal to each other. At her side, like an obedient watch-dog, was the meat-bag who had caused her pain.

The piece of glass still stuck out of his eye because Belial considered it a vast improvement to his appearance and forbade its removal. He was still in the thrall of the angel essence Belial had given to him so he could perform his tasks without the hindrance of any additional pain.

Belial smiled. "I may have some more use for you yet." Mr. Scary grinned stupidly.

The three of them sat in the back of his office behind the famous Hell-Hole amusement ride.

The place had been shut since the last owners went out of business and Coney Island lost most of its attraction. At one time, it had been wildly popular, offering spine-tingling chills and incomparable thrills.

The ride itself was just a circular stand that humans would be held up against by centrifugal force as the false bottom dropped out from beneath their feet. It was supposed to emulate the depth and despair of Hell. If only they knew.

Belial loved Coney Island and had used its ruin and disrepair as a place to conduct his business.

Tonight, it would be the back-drop for settling some long standing scores.

Belial heard the creak of the old wooden floor boards as Mal walked in the back door.

"Is everything ready?" he asked, never turning his way and continuing to thread the coin.

"As ready as we'll ever be," Mal said.

"Good, I'm sure our brothers will be here soon."

CHAPTER THIRTY-ONE

Joe and Nan had a lot to talk about as they drove home.

Mainly, Joe did an enormous amount of apologizing for the fuck-ups of his past and made a lot of promises for their future.

When they were finally home, they walked hand in hand into the cozy house they had shared for more than twenty years. Once inside, Joe knew there was only one thing left for him to do.

"Hey, babe," Joe said, smiling, "how about you make a nice pot of the good coffee and I'll go to LaTorre's Bakery and get some of those mini-pastries you love so much."

"If that's what you want," Nan said, disappointment oozing with each word, "but we still have so much to talk about. Everything that happened today—why us? A lot of things, Joe."

"I know, I know. And, we will, I promise. Just as soon as I get back with the cake. "C'mon," he smiled, "tell me you couldn't go for a cannoli with your coffee?"

"Chocolate?" she asked, grinning like a kid again.

"Is there any other kind?"

Joe started for the basement and Nan's heart skipped a beat. She stared at the floor and with a voice close to tears, said, "That's not the way to LaTorre's."

How could he be so stupid? Joe tripped over the coffee table as he ran to take his wife in his arms. Holding her tight, afraid to let go, he said, "Oh God, Nan. I'm sorry. But you gotta listen to me. I'm through with that shit. Through with the lies, through with all of it."

He held her face in his hands and kissed her eyes, salty from crying.

"I made you a promise to never do drugs again and I'm going to keep it," he said.

"But, the basement... You were—"

"I left my wallet down there. Gotta pay for those chocolate cannolis with something. I know I'm good looking, but Mrs. LaTorre is like 86. Besides, I hear she only puts out cannolis for the younger guys."

Nan started to laugh. It felt so good to laugh again. "I'm sorry, Joe," she began. "I thought—"

"It's okay, Babe. Everything from now on is gonna be okay. I know you have no reason to trust me or anything I say but, I swear, as God is my witness, I won't hurt you again. Okay?" he said, looking and finding forever in her eyes.

"Okay," she answered as they kissed each other long and hard, with a passion neither of them had felt in too long.

"Wow," Joe said with a loving leer, grabbing a quick feel of his wife's round bottom. "Maybe, I'll get the cake later."

"Oh, shut the fuck up and get out of here," she said, playfully pushing him away.

"Alright, but if I'm not back in a while, Mrs. LaTorre has me hostage."

They both laughed as she made her way to the kitchen and he headed towards the basement.

Stopping one last time before he went in, Joe looked at the woman he had loved for almost his whole life and said, "I'll be right back, I promise."

He meant that from the bottom of his heart. The real problem was convincing his head to believe it.

CHAPTER THIRTY-TWO

Michael and Azriel studied Joe's map of the Hell-Hole like generals plotting their next strategic move.

Once Nan and Joe were safe and secure in their car, Azriel and Michael had apparated to this spot and started to wait.

They had been standing on the corner of Stillwell Avenue and 12th St. for the better part of two hours, watching for anyone leaving or entering the building where Maria was being held captive.

The only one they had seen so far was Mal. His huge body was unmistakable.

Many ages ago, Malachi had given up one of his heavenly brothers to Belial, who had already been cast out and living on Earth. Subsequently, Belial tortured and destroyed him.

Malachi was immediately cast out and had his wings taken away. But, anyone who had known Mal or fought with him knew that punishment was exactly what he had wanted.

During the great war in heaven, Mal was primarily absent, waiting in the background to see who would win. He had no preference, one side over the other, but insisted on being part of the winning side. His actions would have gone mostly unnoticed if he hadn't enjoyed killing so much. So, when Belial told him he could kill as many humans as he wanted if he just helped him destroy fellow angels, Malachi thought it was a pretty sweet deal.

Since then, the two expatriates inflicted all types of pain and suffering upon humans. Truth be told, Mal enjoyed the torment even more than Belial because for Mal, there was no reason like vengeance or jealousy involved. No matter who died, he simply enjoyed the destruction. He particularly took great pleasure in their faces. In fact, the only piece of human technology he couldn't live without was a cell phone camera. With it, he would capture all the grotesque, pitiful, last living images of all those he murdered. His phone was so full of these pictures he'd had to purchase something called more memory and have it professionally installed.

"What do you think Mal had in the bag he carried?" Azriel asked Michael as they stood in the shadows of a burnt out building.

"I do not know," Michael replied, "but my guess would be a weapon of some sort."

Azriel looked pensive and worried.

"Do not concern yourself with these things," Michael said, looking once again at the map to see if they missed something.

"I am not worried for myself. God will protect me. I am worried about you, my friend. When the council finds out about this woman, you will be banned from earth or worse—you will become one of the unloved."

"I will handle that problem when the time comes," Michael said, lowering his head as if in prayer. "My only concern is for Maria's safety. I can handle anything that comes afterward as long as she is safe and secure."

Azriel looked at his friend, trying to find a way to ask a question that was on his mind for quite some time. Finally, he simply asked, "What is it like to love a human?"

Michael smiled. "It is impossible to explain," he said, trying to find the right words. "While I have felt the Lord's unwavering love since the beginning, and as an angel I have never been without my brothers, there was still a part of me that was lonely. After eons of watching these souls, I longed for that which I saw. The embrace of someone you love, soft lips pressed against my own, and the physical warmth of being close to someone you care for more than anything else. This is what I experience within Maria's arms. She is everything."

"What about God?" Azriel whispered, afraid someone might hear.

"I love the Lord with all my heart and always will," Michael replied. "I will praise his name and do his work until the end of eternity. But, I refuse to believe that these feelings I have are wrong or forbidden by the one who gave them to me. He is my creator and all that I know and love comes from him. How, then, could my love for Maria not be blessed?"

"I can't say that I understand," Azriel said, looking directly into his friend's eyes, "but I will fight for your right to love as fiercely as I will fight Mal and Belial to return whom you love."

"Thank you, Azriel," Michael said sincerely. "It will not be easy."

"I am ready," Azriel said. "Are you?"

"I have been ready to destroy Belial for ages," Michael replied, a darkness descending upon him. "The real question is, will he be ready for me?"

CHAPTER THIRTY-THREE

Joe turned on the basement light. For a split second, his senses were bombarded with the sins of his past. Too many years had been wasted down here trying to forget his life and forget how he had failed at being a son, a father, and a husband.

He had a lot of making up to do to all those that had suffered because of him. Tonight, he would start.

Joe entered the room that had once been his father's office, the one they had both used to keep an angel prisoner.

The walls were still lined with vials full of forcibly obtained angel essence. Gone, however, was any temptation for the false euphoria or the all-encompassing need to get high on anything.

Scattered haphazardly on the floor were some of Azriel's feathers. He wondered if the damage he had caused the angel would reverse itself and silently prayed that it would. He couldn't bear the idea that he had permanently altered one of God's own.

Standing behind his father's old desk, Joe reached under the middle drawer looking for the hidden key his father had kept there and the one he had discovered so many years ago. He hadn't thought about this key or what it opened in ages, but this seemed like the perfect time to see what was in there and whether or not it could be helpful in the situation.

Once he had the key in his hands, he walked over to the middle of the room, careful not to step on any feathers.

Reaching down, he pulled up the old throw rug, exposing a few wooden floor boards that were a slightly different color from the rest. He then picked up the boards and threw them into the corner.

In the hole that remained, Joe fished out a metal container about the size of a tool box.

The first time he had seen the box in his father's office, he had been sixteen years old. Joe had, once again, gone downstairs to see the angel and experience the euphoria that only the creature could bring.

When he got there, however, the angel was not alone. Belial was down there with his old man and they were arguing.

Joe could remember it all like it was yesterday.

"Listen, Nino, I don't give a damn about your phony Catholic guilt or your reluctance over hurting an angel." Belial was angry. "You knew what you were getting into when I brought him here."

"Who do you think you're talking to?" Nino DeFalco spat, staring at Belial with pure hatred in his eyes. His face had turned a brilliant shade of red and he was shaking. "Do you know who I am?"

"Nino, please spare me your typical Godfather bullshit." Belial casually brushed by him and specifically sat in the old man's leather chair. "I am not one of your guinea soldiers that do whatever you say. I am Belial, fallen from grace and unloved by God. I could end you and your entire line before you could say lasagna.

Belial reached into his breast pocket and pulled out his silver coin. As he played with it in his hand, he continued, "I have been killing your kind since your time began. Now, you can do as I say or you can rest assured your wife will be a widow and your son will be just another headless corpse. Your choice."

"Why you miserable, little cocksucker, motherfucker," Nino DeFalco said in a tone that could turn rain to ice. "I don't care what the fuck or who the fuck you think you are, nobody, and I mean NOBODY, threatens me or mine." Nino pulled the nine millimeter from the side holster he always wore and shot Belial in the chest.

Belial stumbled backwards and began to laugh. "Stupid humans. You never learn." Reaching out, he took the gun from Nino's hand and placed it on the desk between them.

"No matter how many times you are put in your place, you all still believe you are greater than your superiors. You have just signed your own death certificate, Nino. However," he continued, rising from Nino's chair and brushing him aside once again as he walked past him towards the door, "before you die, you will drain that angel until he is no more and give me all the money. If you try anything—anything at all—before that task is complete, I will cut off your beloved son's testicles and shove them down your wife's throat. Do you understand, or should I say *capiche*?"

"Yes, " Nino answered, barely able to breathe and still in shock by what he had just witnessed.

"Good," Belial said, as he walked up the storm cellar stairs. "See that you don't forget. And one last thing, as the characters in one of your favorite movie once said, 'It's not personal, Nino. Strictly business.'"

The heavy metal doors slammed shut but Nino didn't hear them. Instead, he fell to the floor and wept.

Joe watched his father cry for a little while longer before the old man got up, went for the secret key, and opened the locked box. From his vantage point, Joe couldn't see what his father had put in there but he seemed more at peace when he was done.

Now, it was Joe's turn. He opened the box and was immediately struck by an acrid burning smell. Inside, he found his father's nine millimeter, a .45 revolver, and a pump action, sawed off shotgun.

Still searching, he uncovered a dagger wrapped in a very old felt cloth, the likes of which Joe had never seen before. The blade was silver and shined to a pristine luster while the handle was made of a wood he didn't recognize and had a single word chiseled into it. Joe could not make out the word. He was pretty sure it was a very old language and one hundred percent positive that it was way beyond his schooling.

It was far easier to understand the burning smell. As soon as he touched the blade, he pulled his hand back in agony, leaving some of his skin upon it.

Sucking on his wounded finger, Joe kept looking through the box for anything else he could find. On the bottom was an envelope with his name clearly written on it.

He recognized his father's old school cursive and opened it. With shaky hands and a stomach full of nervous butterflies, Joe began to read.

Joey,

If you're reading this, then I'm dead. I'm pretty sure what, or to be more accurate, who killed me, but in the end, make no mistake, it was this stinking lifestyle that did it.

I'm writing this letter to apologize for all I've done, ask for your forgiveness, and give you a warning.

I'm sorry I couldn't be the father you needed. I never wanted my choices to affect you but I know they have.

I also want you to know that I knew it was you that let the angels go. I killed an innocent man to cover for you and I would have killed a million more to keep you safe. What I really should have done was let them go myself. But, I was never that brave and the fear of losing you and your mother to that cocksucker Belial was more than I could bear.

You did good, Joe. People like me talk about our love of God, go to church every Sunday, and even donate money to the church to make up for our multitude of sins.

But some things, like what I done to that angel, are beyond God's forgiveness. I'm not afraid of being damned.

We all get what we deserve, but I want you to remember what this life cost me—my soul. I pray you make better choices for yourself.

I have placed a very old dagger and some guns in my box along with this letter, hoping one day you would find it and learn from my mistakes.

The dagger is special. I had it made from the silver coins Belial's always playing with. Had a couple of my guys rob them from his office safe in Coney and replace them with perfectly crafted duplicates. After all, your old man was never without some gifted friends, and if I was going to take him out, I was going to use something that he loved very much.

I'm leaving this weapon for you in case that fuck-face is still around and you have become involved with him.

If that's what happened, then you fucked up, Joe—big time. So, before he hurts you or those you love, take the motherfucker out.

And, should the dagger fail, use the shotgun to blow his fucking head off. I'm sorry, Joey. Sorry I couldn't be the father you needed or wanted.

I love you, very much. Don't be a fuck-up like me. Take care, kid. Your Pops

P.S. Don't know what those coins are made of but they cost the guy who made the dagger a couple of fingers, so be careful.

Bye, kid.

Joe didn't realize he'd been crying till some of his tears fell on the letter. But he knew why he was crying.

His father was a hard guy. A real prick, some would say. But to Joe, he was just his Pops.

And though he never said I love you out loud, the letter proved what Joe always knew, that his father really did.

Joe put the letter in the back pocket of his jeans, took the dagger covered in its cloth, and grabbed the shotgun.

Walking up the same storm cellar stairs Belial had used so many years ago, Joe's mind was on one thing—revenge.

"Don't worry, Pops, that fuck will pay for everything he's done—I promise."

CHAPTER THIRTY-FOUR

Michael and Azriel walked into the Hell-Hole at the exact time that Belial had instructed. Old-time calliope music was playing over the speakers and the room was lit up with thousands of multi-color blinking lights.

The ride was on and spun around and around on an invisible axis. Michael thought he could make out two figures standing on it, but the ride was going too fast to be sure.

The music, lights, and constant spinning were distracting—probably on purpose—and Michael could tell Azriel was losing focus.

"Pay no attention to the noise," Michael whispered. "Just remember what I told you."

CHAPTER THIRTY-FIVE

Sixteen years ago

Dante's was the most popular bar in Rome. Cool enough to make the European hipsters happy and quiet enough for the serious drinker to get their load on.

For Bub, who tended bar there three days a week, it was a place to meet new people and listen to their individual stories. Bub was a great listener.

"What can I get you?" Bub asked the distinguished looking gentleman who'd just sat down.

"Water," Belial answered, in no mood for conversation with another meat-bag. In the past few years, he had spoken to enough of these rejects to make the prospect of answering a simple question excruciatingly painful. The very idea that any of these humans might ever be able to help him was incomprehensible, but he was at his wits end and was told, over and over, that this bar might be the place to find the answers he needed or the item he'd been searching for.

"Water?" Bub repeated, making sure he had heard the smelly little guy right.

"Yes, water. Why, you got a problem with that?"

"No, no, not at all," Bub replied, displaying a bright and genuine smile. "Just not a common request."

Grabbing a glass of water, Bub placed it in front of his new customer. "So what brings you to Dante's tonight?"

"That's my business. How about you find someone else to annoy?" Belial replied, his disgust growing by the second.

"No problem. Didn't mean to bother you," Bub said. "We just get a lot of people in here who seem to be looking for something—something they can't find on their own, despite their obvious skills. Let me freshen that water."

Belial watched the meat-bag walk away. He wondered, could this piece of trash help him find what he so desperately needed and had searched every corner of this world to locate?

After the deal with Nino had gone bad and the three angels they had captured wore out their usefulness, Belial had been disappointed. Even finding out that his maimed and tortured brethren had all ceased to exist as a direct result of his actions had left him only slightly pleased.

However, after witnessing Michael's agony and guilt over his brothers' deaths, Belial's mood greatly improved. He felt renewed and couldn't wait to catch and drain other angels on earth.

Unfortunately, this unbridled joy was short-lived.

Once Michael started destroying anyone or anything associated with Belial, he knew if he didn't run far and fast, he would soon be next. The archangel would eventually find him, and once that happened, no mercy would be shown.

When he left New York, it was with a definite purpose—to find something or someone to help him get rid, once and for all, of any angels that happened to be on earth, especially Michael.

Belial had searched for more than thirteen years. Starting in Israel, the holy land, through the rest of the middle east and then the orient. In each part of the globe, he had read all the ancient tomes he could find, written on everything from rock to vellum, looking for a clue that would help him eradicate his problem for all time.

Rome, and the Vatican in particular, was his last chance. If he couldn't find what he was looking for among the oldest relics of Christianity in the world, he never would.

"Here ya go," Bub said, placing the cold glass of ice water in front of Belial. Turning to leave, Belial stopped him in mid-step.

"Hold on there, Bub," Belial said, looking at the bartender's name tag. "I might be looking for something. Something very old and important to no one but myself."

"Oh, I don't know about that," the bartender said, an amused smile illuminating his face. "I know what you seek and why you seek it and can tell you, without a doubt, there are many others who also desire it."

"How could you know?" Belial asked. "Who are you?"

"I am no one—NO ONE!" Bub answered, laughing as he spoke. "I'm sorry. Inside joke, an old movie reference. Still makes me laugh. Who I am or how I know is not important. What is important, is our shared interest in what you seek and its intended purpose. I am the only one who can help you."

"What do you want from me in return?" Belial asked, worried for the first time in his existence, about the answer.

"There is nothing you or your kind can give me but there is something you can do for me."

"What would that be?" Belial inquired warily.

"Destroy the archangel," Bub said, his face growing dark and menacing as his eyes burned bright as fire. "That is all I ask of you."

"How can I be sure you have what I need?" Belial asked.

"I think you already know the answer to that, Belial," Bub answered. "Rest assured your search is over. Take a minute and compose your thoughts. I'll get you another water and we'll talk more."

"Where have you been?" Belial asked, earnestly in awe of the figure that stood before him tending a small bar in Rome.

"Nowhere...everywhere. Qui procul ab oculis, procula limite cordis, Latin for 'out of sight, out of mind.' It is how I wish to remain for the time. I will soon remind the world of who I am."

As Bub turned around, Belial came to the realization that he was not surprised. However, he was usually much more observant.

Looking at the bartender yet again, for the first time since he walked into Dante's bar, Belial really saw him. Beautiful face, unblemished skin, long flowing hair, and preternaturally sharp nails, honed to fine points—it really was him.

Bub, short for Beelzebub, was a fallen angel, too. The first fallen angel, the Morning Star.

Belial had hit the jackpot.

CHAPTER THIRTY-SIX

Present Day

Belial walked out of the back room smiling. In his right hand he held a pair of eyes, strung together grotesquely like a macabre key chain.

"I swear, Belial, if you—" Michael began but was immediately interrupted.

"Don't rustle your feathers, brother. They're not hers," Belial sneered. "I like to keep certain souvenirs from other members of the family that get in my way."

"Where is she, Belial?" Michael asked, walking slowly around the right side of the ride as Azriel walked around the left.

"She's here," Belial answered, swinging the eyes round and round his index finger.

"Where? Tell me." Michael moved closer.

"You'll see," Belial said as he reached for a lever sticking out of the wall and pulled it down.

The ride made a loud clanging noise as if it were about to break. Michael watched the ride as it slowly came to a stop. The two figures he thought he had seen before rapidly came into focus.

Michael gasped. Strapped to the ride was his beloved Maria. She was caked in blood and her nose had been broken. Both eyes were blackened and barely open. A glimmer of recognition shone in them when she spotted him but was quickly replaced by a wince of excruciating pain that cut through Michael like a knife.

Michael tried apparating to her side to rescue her, but it wasn't working.

"None of your angel tricks here, Brother," Belial laughed. "This entire room is covered with the ancient symbols that will render you and any of your self-righteous meat-bag lovers powerless."

"But how did—" Michael began, his fury increasing by the second.

"The symbols were written in the blood of the most innocent. But don't worry, they won't miss it. They weren't in this world long enough to miss their remarkably short lives. The symbols themselves come from the first fallen."

"The Morning Star," Michael whispered, shocked by the mere mention of his name.

"Yes, the very first fallen," Belial continued. "He has learned much from his time in Hell, but especially how to hurt those he once trusted and called brother."

"I will destroy you, Belial," Michael said and meant it. "Let her go."

"Oh, I will. I will." Belial smiled in a way that sent chills down Michael's spine. "Have you met Herman?"

Belial asked, pointing to what was left of a man standing in the spot on the ride that was right next to Maria. "We have become quite friendly in the short time since we met, but my understanding is he became particularly friendly with your female meat-bag.

Michael lunged for Belial. Before he could reach him, the unloved pressed a switch on his belt buckle, unleashing a pair of metal wings from a compartment on his back.

They were hideous. An affront to the beauty and majesty of an angel's real wings. The feathers were made of metal and polished to a brilliant hue. Each one came to a razor sharp point at the ends, creating an extremely deadly weapon for anyone who dared to approach the wearer.

Belial flew upwards with a speed that rivaled Michael's own and landed on the balcony overlooking the ride.

"That was stupid, Michael. Very stupid. Try something like that again and Herman will reach over and snap her pretty neck. Won't you, Herman?" Belial asked as what was left of Mr. Scary's face appeared to grin stupidly and nod up and down.

"Good, very good. Now here's what's going to happen. You will take Azriel in the back where I will restrain him, cut off his wings, and drain him of his essence till there is nothing left but a shell of the angel you once knew. And you, Michael, you will watch and do nothing or else Herman will kill your beloved bag of bones without a second thought. Then, and only then, when what was Azriel is no more, perhaps I will give her back to you and you can both leave."

"Do it, Michael," Azriel pleaded. "I am not afraid, and you have no other choice."

"No, but I do." Joe came out of the back office with the sawed off shotgun in his right hand. "You guys didn't think I'd let you have all the fun, did you?"

Belial was incensed. His arms outstretched, he flew to where Joe was standing.

Azriel intercepted him before he could reach Joe and slammed Belial into the lever on the wall.

The ride began to spin again, and the lights and music starting blaring.

Joe picked up the sawed-off weapon and tried to get a good shot at Belial. It was next to impossible as Azriel kept getting in the way.

"Michael, get Maria," Joe yelled.

The ride kept spinning faster and faster and the false bottom began to drop.

Without the ability to apparate, and with the ride still moving way too fast, Michael saw no safe way to save Maria.

"Joe, pull the lever down!" Michael roared above all the noise.

Joe moved to get around Belial and Azriel. Reaching for the lever that controlled the ride, he felt the most pain he had ever felt in his life when an arrow pierced his right hand and pinned him against the wall.

Looking in the direction that the arrow came from, Joe saw Malachi whose arm was pulled back, ready to take another shot with his crossbow.

Joe knew he was about to die when Michael flew between the two of them and took an arrow to his side. He fell to the ground in a heap of feathers, his face contorted by pain.

"Hurts, doesn't it?" Malachi said, taking his cell phone from his pants pocket and preparing to take Michael's picture to add to his collection of those he'd killed. "It should. The wood comes from the Judas tree, the same one God cursed and the only thing on earth that can kill an angel."

Joe knew he had seconds to do something before Malachi ended Michael's existence. Without another thought to the tremendous amount of pain coming his way, he pulled his hand through the arrow that held it, leaving skin and bone along the length of the shaft. Once free, Joe used his left hand to cock the shotgun, pull the trigger, and blow Malachi's head clean off his body.

"Goodbye motherfucker," Joe mumbled before passing out in a pool of his own blood.

Michael was in bad shape. The arrow in his side had damaged the internal organs of his human body. And still the ride went round and round. He knew his time was almost over but he also knew he wasn't going anywhere without saving the only person he'd ever loved.

"God, please," he whispered, "give me strength."

Slowly, Michael got to his feet and moved towards the lever.

Belial saw his chance. Still struggling with Azriel, he reached up with one arm and grabbed the arrow that Mal had shot through Joe's hand. Plunging it deep into Azriel's chest, the angel hit the floor with a sickening thud.

"NOOOOO!" Michael screamed. Within moments, his friend was gone. Any trace of his being vanished from existence.

Michael was on his feet again. In a burst of rage, he flew at Belial, smashing him against the wall. With a ferocity he hadn't felt in a long time, he grabbed Belial by the throat and started to squeeze.

Belial pulled at Michael's hands but could not free himself from the angel's grasp.

"You're mine now," Michael said, spitting the words into Belial's crimson face.

"Not...yet..." Belial barely got the words out. Removing his hands from Michael's, he reached in his pocket, took out his coin, and pressed it against Michael's forehead.

Michael screamed in agony. He had never experienced pain like this before. He let go of Belial and felt a perfect copy of the coin burned into his skin.

Still, the ride continued to spin.

Belial was on his hands and knees, gasping for air.

"Do it, Herman," he managed to get out in a voice he no longer recognized as his own.

Michael heard Maria scream as Mr. Scary untied her restraints and pushed her into the abyss below the ride.

A second later, there was a sickening thud and Michael knew instinctively he was too late.

"Awww, did Herman kill your precious meat-bag? Belial taunted. "These humans can be so violent."

"You have no idea," Joe whispered in Belial's ear as he snuck up behind him and stuck his father's dagger in what should have been Belial's heart. As he pulled it out, Joe gave it a twist for added measure.

"You...can't...kill...me..." Belial struggled for each word. "You're just a meat—"

Belial, the fallen angel, the unloved, disappeared in front of Joe and Michael's eyes.

In tribute, Joe brought up a mouthful of phlegm that only a life-time cigarette smoker could produce and spit it on the ground where Belial had been a second before.

The ride was over and came to a complete stop.

Michael had to see for himself that she was really gone. Had to look upon her sweet, loving face one last time. He tried to get up off the cold, hard ground but fell back down, too weak to move.

He pulled the cursed arrow from his side with one quick move. He was losing his essence rapidly and didn't care. His life with Maria was over and so was his desire to go on.

"Do not move, Michael," a voice he recognized instantly said. "We will get her."

Gabriel and Manakel stood above him.

"How? Why?" Michael tried to ask the questions that entered his thoughts but was having trouble forming coherent sentences.

"Rest now," Gabriel said. "We will accompany her on the remainder of her journey."

"I must see her," Michael insisted, trying to rise again.

"She is gone," Manakel said abruptly.

"You don't understand—"

"We understand more than you know," Manakel interrupted.

"You understand nothing," Michael said quietly, resignation in his voice.

Michael knew asking his brethren how they bypassed Belial's symbols or why they didn't arrive earlier, in time to save Maria, was pointless. They could no more explain God's greater plan for Maria than they could fathom why he loved her so. They just weren't built that way.

Looking at the carnage that surrounded him, Michael spotted Joe on the ground a few feet away.

"Are you alright, my friend?" he asked.

"I think so," Joe replied. His whole body ached as he continued to lose blood. His right arm was useless and hung lifeless at his side. There was a visible hole in his hand where Mal had nailed him with the arrow. His left hand was not much better. While plunging his old man's dagger through that piece of shit Belial was well worth any pain he felt, the blade had burned him irreparably, leaving mangled skin and shards of bone behind.

These things alone were bad enough, but Joe knew his physical pain was nothing compared to what Michael was going through. He didn't know what he'd do if Nan were hurt, or God forbid, killed.

But, he also knew this was not the time to dwell on what-ifs or could-have-beens. He was too busy studying another two angels that had popped into his life.

As he marveled, once again, at the miracle in front of him, one angel disappeared and reappeared in the blink of an eye.

When he returned, there was a beautiful ball of light at the angel's side. It was brighter than anything he'd ever seen, and it gave off an electrical charge that made the hair on Joe's arms stand up. Whatever it was, he was positive the orb was alive.

Michael stared at the orb that Manakel had brought back and wept openly. He knew he was watching Maria's soul and it was every bit as beautiful as she had been.

The orb floated in mid-air, as if suspended by an invisible string. Ever so slowly, it circled around Michael. He lifted his arm and opened his hand. The orb danced above it before settling down in Michael's palm.

His body shook as if electrified. The power of Maria's love emanated from the orb as Michael became one with her soul. A voice that only he could hear said, "Do not grieve. I am fine. My love for you cannot be stopped by death. It will endure till the end of time as will I. We will see each other again, I know it. Till then, stay strong and be happy. I love you, Michael, forever and always."

Michael watched as the soul of the only woman he had ever loved apparated along with Manakel.

"Goodbye, my love," he whispered.

Gabriel looked around at the mess that remained. Malachi's blood splattered cell phone, Azriel's wasted essence, Belial's hideous metal wings and a staggering amount of feathers lost in battle.

"You know what must be done." Gabriel looked at Michael still sitting on the ground.

"I do," he said.

Gabriel reached down to help his friend. "I cannot say I understand what happened here," Gabriel said, looking directly into Michael's eyes, "but the questions will wait for the council. I will pray for you, brother."

Gabriel hugged Michael in a tight embrace. When they separated, he was gone and Michael's physical wounds were healed.

"It is time to go," Michael said, turning to Joe. "But first…" He picked Joe up like a father carries their child. The second they touched, Joe felt the same body consuming tremor he had experienced just hours ago. Once again, he was soothed by the rush of warmth as it continued to spread over every part of his body until he was completely whole and well for a second time today.

When Michael put him down, there were tears in Joe's eyes. "Thank you," was all he could manage to say.

Joe did a quick check on himself, both inside and out. Except for a nasty scar on both sides of each hand, he was completely healed.

"Now what?" he asked, looking around and trying to remember what he had once loved about this place.

"We must destroy any evidence that cannot be explained to a human," Michael replied. "We must burn it down."

Joe and Michael began searching for anything they could use to start a fire. Joe found some gasoline in the back office that, at one time, had been used to power the ride. With Michael's help, they began pouring the fluid on the floors and walls.

When they were done, every part of the building had been doused with the flammable liquid. Taking one last look around, the cost of what had happened in this room was not lost on either one of them.

Lost in their own thoughts, a loud noise interrupted them. They both turned in time to see Mr. Scary/Herman stumble down the steps off the ride.

"What do you want to do?" Joe asked Michael, who stared, devoid of all emotion, at the excrement that had taken away his only chance at true happiness.

"Nothing," Michael finally answered. "Let him be. Consider the things that Belial must have done to him."

Joe thought about Michael's words in silence. He watched as Mr. Scary, whose hand was as badly injured as Joe's had been and whose face no longer resembled anything human, tripped on his own feet and landed on his ass.

"I don't know," Joe said, grabbing a cigarette from the pack in his pocket and putting it in his mouth. "He looks like the kind of guy who enjoys a little suffering between friends."

Mr. Scary smiled that same stupid angel essence induced smile he wore earlier.

"Let him go, Joe." Michael's voice grew louder. "His death will not bring either one of them back."

"You're right, you're right. I know you're right," Joe said, pulling out a book of matches from his pants pocket and lighting his cigarette. "The only problem is...I've always been so fucking wrong."

Joe flicked his lit cigarette at Mr. Scary. He watched as it bounced off him and fell in the pool of gasoline at his feet.

People who lived in Coney Island would later say they heard the gut-wrenching screams of a man the day the Hell-Hole burned to the ground. There just wasn't enough of anything or anyone left in the ashes to prove they were right.

CHAPTER THIRTY-SEVEN

"What will you do now?" Joe asked as Michael parked the Cadillac on the corner of Lake St. and Avenue U.

"I do not know," Michael replied as they both got out of the car. His voice was full of exhaustion and regret. "I have to go before the council."

"What will happen then?" Joe hoped he didn't sound too nervous for his friend.

"I do not know, but I must place my faith in our heavenly Father to decide what is best."

"I thought you were done with sharing one mind and wanted to choose for yourself how you continue your existence?" Joe looked at Michael to see if he had crossed another line.

"It would seem, Joseph," Michael said, fighting to hold it together, "that was not meant to be. Making my own choices cost me the greatest gift I was ever given."

Joe thought about this for a few minutes. "Or maybe," he said, "you would have never met her if you didn't make your own choice. We must all live with the consequences of every decision we make. My father, John, and even that piece of shit Belial all made the wrong choices during their time here. But, I don't know a human being alive who would rather have their freedom taken away because they're afraid of making a mistake." Joe looked at Michael and hoped he was listening. "Our right to choose our own path is what makes love more meaningful and life worth living."

"Thank you, Joe," Michael said, "for everything".

"Will I see you again?" Joe asked, his voice cracking.

"Aren't you tired of angels yet?"

"Oh, I don't know," Joe said and grabbed Michael in a warm embrace. "Yous guys are alright."

The two friends separated and Joe continued, "And you never realize how bad you need one until an angel shows up and changes your life."

"Goodbye, Joseph."

"Goodbye, Michael," Joe said, but the angel was already gone.

Joe opened the passenger side door of the car and retrieved his black leather wallet from the glove compartment.

LaTorre Bakery was across the street and Nan would kill him if he didn't walk in the house with her chocolate cannolis.

Joe never looked both ways when crossing any street and this time was no different. He also never saw the blue Camaro blow the red light on the corner and come straight at him doing 50 mph.

Instead, he felt a strong push against his chest, propelling him backwards where the car missed him by millimeters.

"Will this fucking day never end? Thanks, Mikey," Joseph DeFalco whispered as the first day of his new life began.

Epilogue

The Hell-Hole went up in a glorious burst of multi-color flames just as he knew it would.

Whatever had occurred inside, there was no doubt that a cleansing of this magnitude would follow.

Sitting in a cherry-red, 1969 Camaro Super-Sport, twin turbo, supercharged nitrous breathing monster, across the street from the popular old ride, he waited patiently for the victors—whoever they were—to emerge. In an instant, he had his answer.

Mr. Scary's anguished screams went on for a full minute and a half. It would take a whole lot longer to regain any semblance of rational thought.

"Where am I?" he finally said, turning to face the person in the car with him.

The last thing he remembered was being dumped in a ditch by some nasty bitch and her super-human watch-dog who just happened to have wings. But that couldn't be right. His head was so foggy and he was having trouble recalling anything that came after that.

"You are in my car," the handsome young man with the long black hair said. "We are in Coney Island, in Brooklyn—"

"I know where Coney Island is," Mr. Scary interrupted, growing increasingly angry at his own memory loss. His hands clenched into hard fists as he struggled to restrain himself and not beat the life out of the guy who was speaking.

"How did I get here?"

"That, my friend, is a long story," the driver answered. "One that requires much time and a willingness to believe the impossible. If you can do that, I will explain everything."

Mr. Scary weighed his desperate need to know what had happened to him against his overwhelming desire to rip this asshole's head off.

"Considering the little I do remember about today, I'm pretty certain I would believe just about anything," Mr. Scary replied, knowing something else with a certainty—when he had the answers he needed, he was gonna kill this pretty boy and own, from what he could tell in his seat, a really sweet car.

"Then let's be off," the driver said as he started the car, seemingly without the benefit of a key. "There is much to do and little time to waste."

"Where are we going?" Mr. Scary asked, suddenly wondering if this guy was just another homo looking to suck his cock. "Is it far?"

"Incredibly close for some, impossibly far for others."

"What the hell does that mean? Who the fuck are you?" Mr. Scary asked, genuinely curious.

"I am No One," Bub said with a snicker as they drove away, the muscle car spitting it's fiery nitrous flames. "And it's funny you should mention hell."

The End ... Fuhgettaboutit...

Nola Cancel is a freelance writer and ex-pat New Yorker living with her husband of 30 years in Largo, Fl.

She has written for Women's World Magazine and The St. Pete Times, as well as many other publications.

Her first book, *Anne Rice The Interviews: A Compilation of Interviews with the Iconic Author on Everything from the Writing Process to Her Extraordinary Life*, has been called, 'A must read for any fan of Anne Rice. The broad spectrum questions asked by Nola Cancel give the reader a deeper intimacy into the inner workings and thoughts of the author's mind, even more so than the author's popular Facebook page.' (Amazon reviewer, Books4Life; Dec. 2014)

She is the mother of the undisputed "cutest dog in the world," her English Bull-dog, Chunkie.

43678648R00104

Made in the USA
Middletown, DE
16 May 2017